"You've been strong all day. I promise you I can take a few sniffles..."

Something in Jonathan's tone made Laura crane her neck to see his eyes, which were laced with both concern and humor. She wiped at her face, which was tingling. It was strange, given that she'd just had a meltdown in front of him, but his teasing actually made her feel better. "A few, huh?"

He nodded solemnly, dark eyes dancing. "I do have a younger sister, you know."

"So you've seen your share of sniffles?"

He gave her a lopsided smile. "I've seen my share of sniffles."

She took a breath. She liked knowing that she could fall apart without fear that he'd judge her. She liked knowing that strong emotions wouldn't scare him away.

She leaned into him and whispered, "Thank you."

"You're welcome, Laura," he whispered back, the lopsided grin still in place. "I like seeing you smile."

Jonathan's voice rumbled through her like the bass line of her favorite song.

It was at that moment Laura knew she was in real trouble...

Meghann Whistler grew up in Canada but spent her summers on the beaches of Cape Cod. Before settling down with her rocket scientist husband and raising three rambunctious boys, she worked variously as a magazine writer, a model and a marketing communications manager at a software company. She loves to hear from her readers, who can reach her at www.meghannwhistler.com.

Books by Meghann Whistler

Love Inspired

Falling for the Innkeeper

Visit the Author Profile page at Harlequin.com.

Falling for the Innkeeper

Meghann Whistler

LOVE INSPIRED
INSPIRATIONAL ROMANCE

LOVE INSPIRED®
INSPIRATIONAL ROMANCE

Recycling programs
for this product may
not exist in your area.

ISBN-13: 978-1-335-48834-3

Falling for the Innkeeper

Copyright © 2020 by Meghann Whistler

This edition published by arrangement with Harlequin Books S.A.

For questions and comments about the quality of this book, please contact us at CustomerService@Harlequin.com.

Love Inspired
22 Adelaide St. West, 40th Floor
Toronto, Ontario M5H 4E3, Canada
www.Harlequin.com

Printed in U.S.A.

Therefore if any man be in Christ,
he is a new creature:
old things are passed away;
behold, all things are become new.
—*2 Corinthians* 5:17

For Paul, my happily-ever-after

Acknowledgments

Thank you to my wonderfully supportive parents, whose adventures in Hong Kong loosely inspired some of Laura's backstory. Many thanks, as well, to my agent, Rachelle Gardner, who believed in these characters from the get-go and helped them find a home, and to my editor, Melissa Endlich, who helped me polish this story to a fine shine.

Thank you to my dear friend Anna for her love and support, and to my Monday night stepsisters for their encouragement.

To Kathleen, Michael and Hari—thank you for proving Laura wrong about lawyers.

To my grandmothers, Myrtle and Frances— I miss you both.

To my mother's side of my family, thank you for all the wonderful summers on Cape Cod! I hope you enjoy visiting the inn in this book as much as the one in real life.

Thank you to Paul and the boys for everything. And to God, who continues to work in me— may my words be a reflection of Your love.

Chapter One

Jonathan Masters pulled up in front of The Sea Glass Inn, turned off his GPS and sighed. How had he gotten himself into this? He really didn't want to intrude on a single mother and her young daughter right at dinnertime.

A sixth-year associate at Meyers, Suben & Roe, the top corporate law firm in Boston, Jonathan had left work early to drive to the sleepy Cape Cod town of Wychmere Bay to take care of some new business. This little inn wasn't the new business, of course, but if he could ensure that Carberry Hotels acquired this prime piece of beachfront property, there was a good shot that the luxury hotel chain would hire Jonathan's firm for all its legal needs.

And if Jonathan wanted to make partner, as his mentor, Mike Roe, had told him just a few nights ago, he needed to prove he was a closer.

"You're smart, Masters," Mike had said, "and a hard worker, but frankly, if that's all you've got, you're a dime a dozen."

Although Jonathan generally took criticism well, that had hurt. In his experience, hard work always paid off. It was what had earned him a scholarship to college at SUNY Albany and what had gotten him into Harvard Law. The idea that it might not be enough to get him a partnership was simply...unacceptable.

So, if Mike wanted him to bring in new business, Jonathan would bring in new business. Maybe he wasn't particularly slick or practiced at glad-handing, but if that was what it would take to earn a partnership, he'd learn. He had to.

He stepped out of the car and looked at the little inn. It was two stories high with gray cedar shingles, black window shutters and a hand-painted sign with its name—The Sea Glass Inn—hanging from a wooden post out front. In other words, quintessential Cape Cod.

The inn's location couldn't be better. It sat at the end of a quiet cul-de-sac, nestled behind the dunes of a sweeping, white-sand beach on Nantucket Sound. Rosebushes grew haphazardly around the split rail cedar fence that surrounded the property. In the distance, a flash of green light shone from the lighthouse at the mouth of the nearby harbor. The sound of the surf crashing against the sand was soothing. Aside from a few walks around Boston Harbor in his rare free time, Jonathan had never spent much time by the sea.

He adjusted his tie and cuff links, the expensive ones he wore when he wanted to impress. Not that he expected a single mother to even notice his wardrobe.

But it was like his battle armor. Look the part, play the part. Get. It. Done.

There were lights on inside the inn, which was a good sign. He left his suitcase in the car, took a deep breath, walked up the brick-lined path to the front door and knocked.

Almost immediately, the door swung open onto a deserted sitting room with a unique sea glass chandelier, and Jonathan was baffled for a split second until he glanced down and saw a dark-haired slip of a girl with a mischievous smile and gigantic green eyes. She was wearing white tights with purple stars, a pink tutu and—of all things—an itty-bitty Red Sox jersey. Plus, she was holding a couple of crumpled twenty-dollar bills in her hand.

Her big eyes went bigger as she focused on his face. "You're not the pizza man," she said, her words betraying just a tiny hint of a lisp.

"Nope." He grinned and crouched down so he was at eye level with her. "Not the pizza man." He peered into the room behind her. "Is your mom around?"

"Emma, honey!" a woman called out, pushing her way through a set of swinging doors into the room. "I told you not to—" She stopped abruptly when she caught sight of Jonathan.

Although he was certain they'd never met—he'd have remembered a face like hers—the sense of familiarity he felt upon looking into her soft green eyes was jarring. Her clear, heart-shaped face was framed by thick dark hair that tumbled over her shoulders and down her back in waves. She was slender and dressed casually in jeans and a Red Sox sweatshirt. Although she had hardly a lick of makeup on her face, he was still almost dazzled by how beautiful she was.

He gave his head a small shake—*don't be an idiot!*—straightened up and offered his hand. "Hi, I'm Jonathan Masters with Meyers, Suben & Roe. I spoke with your mother, Eleanor, earlier about staying here for a few days while we work out the terms of the deal."

"You spoke with my mother…about a deal…?" The green-eyed beauty made no move to come closer and shake his hand.

Oh, man, Jonathan thought ruefully. He'd gotten the sense during his meeting with Eleanor Lessoway, this woman's mother, that Eleanor might be a little flaky—rich, but flaky—but this was taking flakiness to new heights. He wasn't just *intruding* on this woman and her daughter; he was *ambushing* them. And he didn't like it one bit.

"Mommy, he's wearing clothes like Daddy's!" The little girl's voice was filled with excitement.

"Emma, shh." The woman stepped forward and put a hand on her daughter's shoulder. "Why don't you go in the dining room with Aunt Chloe?"

"But he looks just like Daddy!" The girl peered up at Jonathan. "Do you know my dad?"

He shook his head. "I'm sorry. I don't think so, kiddo."

She pushed her lower lip out in a clear pout. It was adorable, and he had to fight to keep a straight face.

"Go in the dining room with Aunt Chloe," her mom ordered, giving her a gentle push in the right direction. After one last piteous look at Jonathan, the girl scampered off.

The woman shot Jonathan an apologetic look. "I'm sorry. Her father wears suits. She only sees him a couple of times a year on video chat."

"Don't worry about it." He smiled at her, hoping to put her at ease. "I didn't catch your name."

"Laura."

"Laura," he repeated. "It's nice to meet you, Laura." This time, when he held out his hand, she shook it, her soft hand warm and delicate in his. He was struck again by how beautiful she was.

"So, you spoke with my mother? About some kind of deal?"

"Just a small legal matter," he said, once again trying to ease her mind.

"A *legal* matter?" Laura repeated. "Is this about the will?"

Jonathan knew that Eleanor and her daughter had just inherited The Sea Glass Inn from Eleanor's recently deceased mother, but he hadn't actually seen a copy of the will. He and Eleanor had simply talked about what kind of offer Carberry Hotels might be prepared to make on the property. "Nothing like that. I have a client—a potential client—who's interested in buying this place."

"You're a real estate agent?" She sounded skeptical.

He gave her a lopsided grin. "Worse. A lawyer."

Her gaze frosted over. "This inn's not for sale."

"Your mother led me to believe otherwise. She invited me to stay for a few days while we work out the terms of the deal."

Laura threw her hands in the air. "She's not even here! She's still in Boston!"

A second woman, a short, sloe-eyed blonde in ripped jeans and a polka-dot blouse, poked her head into the room. "What's going on out here?"

"Nothing," Laura said. "Mr. Masters was just leaving."

"What? No, I—"

But Laura's hands were on his shoulders, and she *literally* pushed him out the door. "Sorry we can't help you," she said, not sounding sorry at all. "Goodbye."

Laura paced on the inn's back patio, oblivious to the sun as it sank low over the sea behind her, her cell phone held tightly to her ear. "I don't understand why you sent a lawyer here, Mom. It's not like we can sell before we fulfill the stipulation set out in Gram's will."

"Oh, darling," her mother said dismissively. "Those are just pesky details."

Laura bit back a sigh. "It's not just details, Mom. Besides, I thought you didn't even want to stay for the whole summer. I thought you wanted to go straight back to Hong Kong."

Laura's parents had lived in Hong Kong for eleven years, ever since Laura was fourteen and was "just the right age for boarding school," and her mother had the whole expatriate thing down pat. Her parents lived in a sprawling, four-bedroom apartment with a sweeping view of Hong Kong's Victoria Harbor, and they ate out every single night. They had a live-in housekeeper who cooked them a full English breakfast every morning and threw together gourmet salads for her mother's lunch. When Laura's two sisters were younger, they'd also employed live-in nannies for each girl.

Although her father had originally accepted a two-year job contract, her parents loved their lifestyle over there so much that Laura wasn't sure they were ever coming back.

Which was all the more reason for her to convince her mother to stay at The Sea Glass Inn until Labor Day so they could meet Gram's crazy stipulation that the two of them run the inn together for a full summer. If they met that condition, the inn would be theirs, and Laura would have a shot at keeping Gram's legacy alive. If they didn't, it would go to Wychmere Community Church, which her grandmother had attended faithfully for the last forty-odd years.

The Sea Glass Inn was the only home Emma had ever known. It was practically the only real home *Laura* had known, also. It was where she'd spent her holidays and summers during boarding school and her first two years of college, before she'd dropped out after marrying Conrad Walker.

It was also where she'd lived ever since her divorce.

The thought of losing The Sea Glass Inn made her sick to her stomach—even if it *had* become a bit of a money pit since the big nor'easter that had hit Cape Cod last year.

"I did, darling," her mother responded airily to Laura's question about returning to Hong Kong. "I do want to get back to your father as soon as humanly possible. But this is Carberry Hotels we're talking about. If anything could change my mind about fulfilling your grandmother's ludicrous stipulation, it would be Carberry Hotels."

Laura watched as a flock of sandpipers ran across the wet sand down by the waves. "What's the big deal about Carberry Hotels?"

Her mother gasped. "Don't you read the paper, darling? Carberry Hotels is one of the top luxury hotel brands in the world. This isn't a measly million or two we're talking about. This offer promises to be *significant*. The least you can do is show the man the kind of hospitality The Sea Glass Inn is known for."

Laura shook her head in disbelief, although she knew her mother couldn't see her. Until Gram's funeral last week, Eleanor hadn't visited The Sea Glass Inn once since she'd deposited Laura on the steps of her boarding school and hopped on a plane to Hong Kong eleven years earlier. She had no idea what kind of hospitality was on offer at the inn these days.

"Why aren't *you* here to entertain him?" Laura demanded.

"Oh," her mother said flippantly, "I'm staying at the Ritz-Carlton in Boston for a few days to catch up with some old friends. You can handle it, can't you, darling? Just show him around a little, and let him know what a fantastic deal Carberry Hotels would be getting if they decide to move forward with the inn."

It was on the tip of her tongue to tell her mother that no, she wouldn't handle it, she didn't want to sell the inn to anyone, let alone a luxury hotel chain that would be sure to bulldoze it, when she realized that if her mother wanted to sell, it meant she'd have to stay for the summer. Which would give Laura a lot more time to convince the woman to let her take over the inn.

"Okay, Mom," she said. "I'll handle it."

"Good girl, darling. Good girl."

The wind gusted, and the long grass waved wildly on the dunes. Laura remembered playing hide-and-seek on this beach with her sisters when they were little, waiting to hear the tinny music of the ice-cream truck as it rolled into the parking lot at the top of the rickety wooden boardwalk. She remembered catching sand crabs and carrying them around in buckets. She remembered sifting through seaweed to collect sea glass, and daring her sisters to touch the remains of washed-up horseshoe crabs.

She turned away from the beach and surveyed the outside of the building. After her divorce, she and Emma had moved in to help her grandmother with some of the more physically and mentally taxing aspects of running the inn.

At twenty rooms, it was bigger than a bed-and-breakfast, but it had the same kind of appeal. Clean and cozy rooms, a sunny dining room, where guests enjoyed their continental breakfast, and a spacious parlor where guests shared stories after a day spent exploring the dunes, walking out on the jetty or lolling around on Sand Street Beach.

The inn did good business during the summer, but it was open only three and a half months out of the year. Even if they had an extremely profitable summer, Laura doubted they'd make enough money to pay for all the repairs that were necessary since last year's nor'easter—especially the repairs to the roof.

Trying to figure out how to keep the inn from falling apart without going bankrupt in the process was keeping her up at night. But the thought of losing it altogether, which she hadn't even considered a possibility until she and her mother had met with the executor of her grandmother's estate last week, was the stuff of nightmares.

She went inside to the dining room, which featured a wood-beamed ceiling and framed nautical posters on the walls, and found her friend Chloe sitting at the end of one of the long communal tables, eating pizza with Emma.

"He still out there?" Laura asked, gesturing to the filmy white curtains covering the windows that faced the street. Last she'd checked, Jonathan Masters's car—a black BMW—had been parked out front, and he'd been pacing up and down the street, phone at his ear.

Chloe nodded. "Still there."

Laura sighed. "Great. That's just great."

"What'd your mom say?"

"Apparently Carberry Hotels wants the inn, and they're prepared to make us a 'significant' offer."

"But that's good, isn't it?" Chloe asked, responding to Laura's less-than-enthusiastic tone. "At least then you'd get some money out of the whole thing, right? If your mom leaves and the inn goes to the church, you get nothing."

"I don't want money," Laura insisted. "I want to keep Gram's legacy alive. I want Emma to be able to stay in the only home she's ever known. I want to do something with my life, build something for our future."

Emma finished her pizza and, for the umpteenth time that day, started singing her favorite song. "Yankee Doodle went to town, riding on a pony…"

Laura used a baby wipe to clean tomato sauce off her daughter's face and added a surprise ending. "Stuck a feather in his cap and called it spaghetti!"

Emma giggled helplessly, shaking her head. "No, Mom! Not spaghetti!"

"Oh, lasagna, right? Stuck a feather in his cap and called it lasagna!"

Emma let her head roll back so she was looking at the ceiling. "No, no, no, Mom! You're so silly! Not lasagna! Macaroni! He called it macaroni!"

"*I'm* silly? *You're* silly!" She tickled Emma and made her squeal in delight. "Come on, honey, do you want to watch a cartoon?"

"Yeah!"

Laura took her into the parlor and cued up a kids' show on the TV. She propped the swinging door open and went back into the dining room with Chloe.

"She told me the lawyer looks like her dad," Chloe said.

Laura snorted. "Well, it's not like she has the best idea of what the man looks like anyway. Five minutes of video chatting on Christmas and her birthday is hardly enough for a four-year-old to have a clear mental picture of her father."

Chloe scrunched her nose in disgust. "I'm sorry, but I never liked him."

"Sadly, that makes one of us."

Chloe leaned forward and placed her hand on Laura's forearm. "You couldn't have known."

"I knew he wasn't that committed to church. I knew he was very ambitious. I should have realized that our priorities weren't aligned. I shouldn't have let him talk me into getting married so fast."

She'd heard that women gravitated to men who were like their fathers, and that had definitely been true in her case. Her father was the managing director of the Hong Kong division of a global management consulting firm. All through her childhood, he'd worked *at least* eighty hours a week and rarely taken time off. The fact that Conrad had been similarly driven should have been a huge red flag, and yet she'd been smitten almost from the moment they met, and had married him a mere six months later.

"Hindsight, right?" Chloe asked.

Laura shrugged. "I learned my lesson. I'm never getting involved with a guy like that again."

"Okay, but are you going to get involved with *any* guy again? It's been almost five years, Laura. You know your grandmother would be doing cartwheels up there if you found someone nice…"

"I have more important things to think about than dating, Chlo."

"I know, but you're not going to meet anyone if you don't put yourself out there. Let me set up a profile for you on that Christian dating site—"

Laura arched a brow. "Because you've had such stunning success with it?"

Chloe laughed. She'd been on more bad dates than anyone they knew. "At least I'm trying."

"If it was just me, maybe," Laura said, shrugging. "But I've got Emma to think about…"

"So no to dating apps. But I could set you up with one of Brett's friends—"

Laura shook her head. "I already know all your brother's friends, and I'm just not ready right now. My heart wouldn't be in it."

Chloe gave a long-suffering sigh. "Fine." She narrowed her eyes and shook her finger at Laura. "But don't think I'm going to drop the subject forever. You're too young to give up on love. And Emma needs a good male role model in her life."

As if on cue, her daughter called out, "Mom! The show's over!" At the same time, there was a knock at the door.

"You mind getting Emma ready for bed?" Laura asked.

"Of course not," Chloe answered.

Chloe took Emma upstairs, and Laura opened the door for Jonathan Masters.

This time, he was carrying a suitcase.

He was probably six or seven years older than she was and five or six inches taller, with dark hair, dark eyes and a runner's build. He had gel in his hair— just enough to keep it in place—and cuff links in his sleeves. His black suit, like the black car parked at the curb, looked expensive, and his red tie, which was slightly askew, highlighted two spots of high color on his cheeks.

It was late in the day, so he had a bit of a five o'clock shadow going on, and just the very faintest hint of a cleft in his chin. He was very good-looking, if you liked that clean-cut, corporate kind of look.

Which Laura did. A lot.

Much to her chagrin.

"So, hello again," she said, not sure if she sounded awkward or sarcastic. In light of his kind eyes and easy smile, she wasn't sure which she'd prefer. "We're not normally open for guests this time of year, but please, by all means, come in."

She'd expected him to look smug when she let him back in, but he didn't. Instead, he looked almost… relieved.

He stepped into the parlor and glanced around. "Where's your mini me?"

"Emma? She's getting ready for bed."

He looked at his watch, not his phone, and Laura's estimation of him crept up a notch. She liked people who weren't always glued to their cell phones. "It's seven thirty."

She raised an eyebrow. "She's four."

"So, not a night owl?"

She laughed at his wry tone. He grinned. She wished he wasn't quite such a good-looking man. It was distracting, and she didn't need any distractions in her life right now. Not when she had to figure out how to convince her mother to stay for the summer without signing the inn over to Carberry Hotels.

Remembering her manners—which she actually did have, despite the fact that barely an hour ago she'd literally pushed this guy out the door—she asked, "Can I get you anything? Water? Coffee? Leftover pizza?"

His eyes lit up. "You have pizza?"

"Sure." She nodded for him to sit on one of the light blue couches in the parlor. "We have cheese or—wait for it—cheese."

He laughed. "I guess I'll take cheese."

She retrieved a few slices for him from one of the inn's three fridges and microwaved them. She gave him his pizza, Chloe came down and said her good-byes, then Laura went upstairs to say good-night to Emma. From the second floor, she could overhear the sounds of Chloe and Jonathan talking, although she couldn't make out any of the words.

When she came back to the parlor, Chloe was gone and Jonathan was standing up, examining a newspaper clipping that was framed and propped up on the mantel.

"My grandfather," she said. "He was a Korean War vet."

He inclined his head. "Respect."

She nodded and sat on the couch opposite from his, wondering how he saw the space. She loved this room. She'd helped her grandmother remodel and redecorate it shortly after Emma was born.

They'd knocked out the back wall and replaced it with huge plate glass windows on either side of a sliding glass door that opened onto a wraparound porch, where guests could sit and watch the sunset over the ocean. Then they'd painted the remaining walls a creamy blue, fixed a seascape over the fireplace and found a battered treasure chest that they filled with sea glass, which the children staying at the inn could add to or take from as they pleased.

She and her grandmother had made the sea glass

chandelier in the entryway themselves, painstakingly hand wiring hundreds of pieces collected over Laura's lifetime. It had taken them two years to finish it. The only thing she took more pride in than that chandelier was her daughter.

Jonathan sat, took his last bite of pizza and nodded to the TV, where Emma's cartoon was paused, a sea of smiling animal superheroes staring out at them. "What are we watching? The animal channel?"

Laura laughed. "Yeah, their new animated programming."

His lips quirked into an easy smile.

"You don't have kids, do you?"

He held up his left hand and wiggled his bare ring finger. "Nope. Not married, either." Then he glanced at *her* ring finger. "I take it there's no Mr. Laura hiding under the eaves?"

"Lessoway," she said. "And no, I went back to my maiden name after the divorce."

"You look too young to be divorced."

She lifted an eyebrow. "And you look too old not to be married."

He laughed and held a hand to his heart as though he'd been shot. "Oh, walked right into that one, didn't I? Sorry. None of my business."

She shrugged, but she was smiling. "It's fine. I'm not offended."

"So, this cartoon your daughter was watching. Let me guess. Animal superheroes trying to convince kids to save the environment?"

She shook her head. "Actually, it's a Bible-based show."

"Ah," he said. "Interesting."

There was something in his tone that gave her pause. She slanted a glance at him. "You're not a Christian?"

He laughed. "I am on Christmas and Easter."

"Oh." She felt a twinge of disappointment, although she wasn't sure why. "Right."

"I take it you are? A Christian, I mean."

She nodded. "My grandmother's influence."

He blinked, the relaxed, teasing manner gone. "Ah, well, that's…nice."

In Laura's experience, young professionals tended to shy away from any mention of faith, as though spirituality might be contagious. Laura knew the truth, though. Before she'd found her faith as a teenager, she'd been a mess: a good girl who'd been abandoned by her own family, a good girl who hadn't been good enough. She thanked God every day that her grandmother's church community had embraced her and helped her see the truth of her identity as a child of God.

She looked at the man sitting across from her and smiled gently. "*Nice* doesn't even begin to describe it."

When she saw that he was at a loss for how to reply, she took pity on him, gave her hands a brisk clap, stood up and said, "Let me show you to your room."

Chapter Two

Jonathan sat on the queen-size bed in his neat, compact room. It didn't surprise him, this room, with its serviceable white bedding, creaky hardwood floors and small beige bathroom with its low showerhead. There was a medium-size flat-screen TV mounted on the wall opposite the headboard and a wooden dresser with sticky drawers. Hanging over the dresser was a watercolor beachscape, the kind you might find in a local art gallery. On the bedside table sat a Bible.

Even the water stain on the ceiling didn't surprise him, indicating that there was probably a leak when it rained. He remembered how badly Cape Cod had been battered during last year's big nor'easter, and the thought of a single mom, her young daughter and her elderly grandmother riding it out alone didn't sit well with him.

Jonathan couldn't stop kicking himself for the way his conversation with the beautiful innkeeper had ended. "Nice?" he said out loud. "You told her her religious beliefs are *nice*?"

He was an idiot.

The truth was, he'd been raised in a Christian home. His mother had taken him and his sister to church with her every Sunday. Their father, on and off mood-stabilizing medication for his bipolar disorder throughout most of Jonathan's childhood, had almost always stayed home.

As a kid, he'd enjoyed church. Sunday school was fun, and each week there was a big potluck in the hall after the service. He'd gorge himself on muffins and macaroni, Jell-O and corn bread, cookies and cake. In the warm months, he and his friends would then spend the afternoon playing by the creek. In the winter, they'd build Lego forts in his friend Pete's basement.

As he'd gotten older, though, and more focused on earning a scholarship, he'd come to see church as little more than time spent away from achieving his goals.

And his goals had been so important to him back then, so all-consuming. He supposed they still were, although lately he'd been feeling…tired. He'd even started wondering if earning a partnership was really going to be enough to make him happy for the long haul.

He'd always had this idea that if he could just reach that brass ring, if he could just grab it and hold on, that would be the thing that would make everything in his life work the way it was supposed to, the thing that would make everything okay.

But would it? Would it really?

Making partner wouldn't magically fix his father's illness. Making partner wouldn't change the fact that he'd been a scared, bullied kid. Making partner wouldn't mean that his father, who'd gone missing when Jonathan was just seventeen, would ever come home.

He gave his head a little shake. He knew his mentor, Mike Roe, wouldn't like this train of thought.

But then he thought about Mike's life: the penthouse apartment and the fancy sports cars, the top-rated restaurants and the best tailored suits. Jonathan used to think Mike's life was what success looked like—and maybe, for some people, it did—but what about Mike's high-maintenance ex-wife? What about the kid he never saw? What about the fact that he had more money than he could spend in a lifetime and he still spent every waking moment at work?

Was this some kind of early midlife crisis? Jonathan wondered. What would he even do with himself if he didn't have this job?

He drummed his fingers on the bedside table. What was with him tonight? He was wildly unfocused, and it was messing with his head.

It was the woman—Laura. She'd thrown him off balance with her beauty and her wit and her kind, gentle smile. Just thinking about her emerald green eyes—which could, by turns, be sharp or playful or kind—made him feel…strange. Whimsical.

And Jonathan never felt whimsical about women. He was more practical than romantic. Back when he'd started at Harvard Law, he'd made a decision not to get distracted by a serious relationship until he made partner, and he'd stuck to his resolution all these years.

He always kept his promises—to others and to himself. After growing up with his unpredictable father, he was very disciplined that way.

Still, he couldn't ever remember feeling drawn to a woman the way he felt drawn to Laura, and it made him wish that circumstances could be different. That he could be here just to get to know her, instead of here to close a deal.

But that was just wishful thinking, and he didn't have time to indulge in frivolity like that. He was here to earn his partnership, period. Here to do due diligence on Carberry Hotels's acquisition of this inn.

If he brought Carberry Hotels on as a client, he'd be a hero at Meyers, Suben & Roe. But if he didn't deliver, he had no doubt it would be only a matter of time before he was shown the door.

Up or Out was the motto of practically every one of the big law firms in the country. If your star wasn't rising, it was falling. Ever since Mike had told him he was "a dime a dozen," Jonathan had felt the clock ticking.

He had only so much time to turn things around.

When Jonathan came downstairs the next morning, he wasn't sure what to expect. He had his suit on, ready to review the inn's contractual obligations, including property contracts, mortgage contracts, supplier agreements and food and beverage licenses. He also wanted to review the inn's business plan and its financial and tax positions.

Not that any of his findings would matter that much to Carberry Hotels—well, Connor Carberry, specifically, the one who was driving this deal. Connor had been on the lookout for a suitable property for months, and nothing had fit the bill. When Jonathan had called him about The Sea Glass Inn, he'd immediately declared it perfect and wanted to move forward with his plan to build a luxury beachfront resort right away.

Jonathan and Connor had been roommates at Harvard, sharing an apartment in a redbrick walk-up halfway between Harvard and Porter Squares. Jonathan had been at the law school while Connor pursued his MBA.

They'd lost touch after graduation. Jonathan had thrown himself into work while Connor had done pretty much the exact opposite, absconding to Europe and Vegas and Dubai. He'd come home about a year ago after a fight in a nightclub that had put him in the hospital, and he was determined to make things right with his dad. Buying and tearing down The Sea Glass Inn and the homes surrounding it to make way for the new resort was, according to Connor, the key to making that reconciliation happen.

It had been beyond perfect that Eleanor Lessoway and The Sea Glass Inn had fallen into Mike Roe's lap—and then been delegated straight to Jonathan due to his relationship with Connor. He still wasn't exactly sure how Eleanor had ended up talking to Mike, although he suspected the fact that Eleanor's husband was a bigwig at a global management consulting company that had the law firm on retainer probably had something to do with it.

Regardless, he wasn't going to look a gift horse in the mouth, especially in light of the report he'd just gotten from the private investigator he'd hired to try to find his father. The report that indicated it was possible that, if Jonathan's father was still alive, he was living on Cape Cod.

But he'd think about that later, after this deal was all wrapped up.

Jonathan smelled coffee and followed the scent through the swinging doors from the front parlor into the dining room, with its two large farmhouse tables and a sideboard holding a pot of coffee.

"Hello?" he called out.

He heard running water and pushed through another door into the kitchen. Laura was at the sink, earbuds in, head bopping to a beat and lips mouthing lyrics to a song he couldn't hear. Even first thing in the morning, no makeup on, hair in a messy ponytail, the woman was gorgeous. He could stand here watching her lip-synch all day long.

Somehow, though, he doubted she'd appreciate that, so he cleared his throat. Her eyes flew open as she pivoted away from the sink, water dripping from her hands to the yellowed linoleum floor.

"Oh, hey." She pulled out her earbuds.

"Sorry. Didn't mean to startle you."

"No worries," she said, stacking a plate on a full drying rack. "Just cleaning up."

"No dishwasher?" he asked, looking around the dated kitchen, again not feeling particularly surprised.

She sighed. "We have one, but it stopped working a few months ago, when Gram got really sick. Whenever I try to use it, it backs up into the sink and sprays dirty water from that thingy," she said, pointing to the air gap cover at the corner of the sink, "onto the floor."

"Want me to take a look?"

She gave him a skeptical glance, her eyes raking pointedly over his suit and tie. "That's okay," she said. "I'll get around to calling a plumber one of these days."

Her quick dismissal of his handyman skills irritated him, although he knew that had he been almost any other associate from his firm, her assessment probably would have been spot-on.

"Do you have time to go over the list of documents I need from you?" he asked. His voice came out gruffer, more demanding, than he would have liked.

She pursed her lips. "Uh, not really. Not right now. Emma's going to get up any minute, and we're pretty much flat-out busy all day."

He blinked. Was she serious? "All day?"

"We've got a playdate in the morning, and then I'm meeting someone for lunch."

"What about after lunch? I can't draw up the letter of intent to purchase until I have a better idea of exactly what we're looking at here."

She shook her head. "I have some work to do this afternoon."

"But I need those documents to get started on *my* work."

She shrugged. "So give me the list. I'll see if I can find them when I have time."

"This is time sensitive," he pressed. "When can you get to it?"

"I don't know!" she burst out, then immediately added, in a significantly calmer voice, "This was all a big surprise to me, so I'm just not sure when I'll be able to help you. Maybe it would be best for you to come back when my mom's back in town."

No way was he heading back to Boston without putting this deal to bed, or at least making some good headway toward that end. His job—his whole future— was on the line. "Laura, look, I'm sorry for springing this on you. I understand it's a hassle. Whenever you have time to get to it will be fine."

She studied him, lips once again pressed into a thin line. "Okay."

He held up his briefcase. "You mind if I set up shop in the dining room?" If he couldn't work on the doc-ument review for *this* deal, there was plenty of other work he could do.

She shrugged. "Knock yourself out."

He went into the dining room. She followed him, watching him take his laptop and a couple of file fold-ers out of his briefcase.

"Help yourself to coffee," she said. "It's fresh."

"Thanks." He poured himself a cup, then looked at her. "You want any?"

"Already had some."

He put the pot down. "Okay."

He sat and shuffled some papers around. He felt awkward. This was an inn, but it was also her *home*, and he felt like a graceless jerk who'd bumbled his way in.

"There's cereal, if you want it," she said. "Or toast."

"I don't usually eat breakfast unless I run first."

"You run every day?" she asked.

Jonathan nodded. "Usually, yeah. Weekends, I mix

it up. Add some high-intensity weight training at the gym."

She gave a mock shudder.

"What's wrong with weight training?"

She gave him an apologetic smile. "Sorry, it was my ex. You'd think he'd joined the Marines, the way he went on about his weight lifting regimen."

He laughed. A lot of the guys at the gym were like that. They took themselves—and their workouts—*way* too seriously.

"If it helps," he said conspiratorially, "I like running better."

Her eyes skimmed over his business attire again, although this time they were teasing rather than dismissive. "Well, then, I hope you brought a change of clothes."

The swinging doors into the dining room opened, and Laura's daughter—even cuter than she'd been the night before—pushed her way in.

Her eyes went huge when she saw him. "You're here! You're still here!" the little girl exclaimed.

"Honey, this is Mr. Jonathan. He'll be staying at the inn with us for a few days."

Emma came right up to him and did a pirouette. She was a slight kid, small and lean, but scrappy somehow. Feisty and full of energy. She reminded him of his sister's dog when they were growing up—a Chihuahua named Tiny Mouse.

"Do you like to dance, Mr. Jonafin?"

"Um…sometimes." He couldn't help it, his eyes flicked to Laura when he answered.

"I love to dance." Emma did another twirl.

"Do you like dogs?" he asked her.

"Dogs are cute!"

"Ever seen a Chihuahua?"

She scrunched up her face in confusion. "A chi-who-wa?"

He pulled out his phone, tapped the dog breed into Google, found a picture and showed it to her.

"Ohhhhhhh," she sighed. "I love her! She's so cute!"

"I had a dog like that growing up. Want to know her name?"

Emma bobbed up and down, nodding.

He grinned. "Her name was Tiny Mouse. We called her Tiny."

"Tiny! 'Cause she's little and cute!"

"You kind of remind me of her," he said.

Emma's eyes went big again. "I do?"

He nodded solemnly. "You do."

"Because *I'm* little and cute?"

He reached out, bopped her lightly on the nose. "Exactly."

She beamed. "What do you like better, Mr. Jonafin? Macaroni or spaghetti?"

"Hmm." He pretended to think for a moment. "Spaghetti. With meatballs."

"Just like Yankee Doodle, Mom!"

"I thought Yankee Doodle liked macaroni," Laura said.

"Nooooo." Emma shook her head emphatically. "Spaghetti. Definitely spaghetti."

Jonathan raised an eyebrow at Laura. She smiled and gave him a helpless shrug.

Emma tugged on his hand. "Can I sing 'Yankee

Doodle' for you, Mr. Jonafin? I really wanna sing 'Yankee Doodle.'"

"What are you waiting for, Tiny?" He rubbed his hands together in a show of anticipation. "Let's hear it."

"Was it weird?" Chloe asked. "Having him there overnight?"

Laura and Chloe were sitting on the patio at Half Shell, the high-end seafood restaurant Chloe and her brother, Brett, had inherited when their parents died. It was lunchtime, but since it was only mid-April, it was still the off-season, and the restaurant wasn't open for business. They were there to talk about the new website Laura was building for Half Shell, which they'd discussed over a couple of burgers that Brett had whipped up while giving Emma an age-appropriate "cooking lesson" in the kitchen. These so-called lessons usually entailed Brett doing the cooking and Emma licking spoons.

Half Shell was located right on the harbor, and although there was still a chill in the air, the sky was dazzlingly clear, the water a slow-churning blue gray. Sailboats and motorboats and even a few commercial fishing boats bobbed in the harbor. Seagulls sculled and screamed overhead. The green light at the end of the jetty flashed faithfully, and Laura chewed on her lip, still trying to reconcile the guy who'd pushed her to find his documents with the one who'd come up with a silly nickname for Emma.

"Was it weird having a guest at The Sea Glass Inn?" Laura parroted back at Chloe. "Um, you do realize that's what the inn is for, right? Having people stay over?"

"Yes, but not during the off-season. He could be an ax murderer for all you know!"

Laura shook her head in amusement. "He's *not* an ax murderer."

"That's what they said about Ted Bundy."

"Also not an ax murderer, Chlo."

Chloe plucked at the large vintage brooch on her jacket, her expression earnest and a little bit concerned. "You get what I'm saying, though, right?"

Laura smiled at her friend reassuringly. "I do, but it wasn't weird—aside from him not knowing what to do with the fact that I'm a Christian and wanting me to fetch him all kinds of documents at the drop of a hat. But otherwise he's perfectly nice, and great with Emma."

Chloe gaped at her. "You let him spend time with Emma?"

"I didn't leave my four-year-old daughter with some random stranger, if that's what you're asking. But when he came downstairs to get coffee this morning, he let her sing 'Yankee Doodle' to him seventeen times."

Chloe's eyes bugged out. "He did?"

Laura took a sip of water to hide her smile. "He did."

"Wow. He looked so…businesslike last night. I wouldn't have guessed he liked kids."

"I know, right?" Laura giggled. He *had* looked a little helpless and panicky by the end of Emma's protracted serenade. Laura had finally taken pity on the man and told her daughter that they had to let "Mr. Jonafin" get on with his day.

"You still good with me taking the squirt to that movie this afternoon?" Chloe asked.

"Sure. It'll give me a chance to do as my mother wanted me to do and 'show our guest around a little.'" Laura put those last few words in air quotes.

Chloe gave her friend a long look.

"What?"

"You like him, don't you?"

"I don't *dislike* him," Laura said slowly.

"But…?"

Laura pushed a strand of dark hair back from her face. "But he represents a client who wants to tear down the inn. So, forgive me if I'm not exactly jumping for joy that he's a decent conversationalist."

"Not bad to look at, either."

Laura threw her friend the stink eye. "Chloe…"

Her friend laughed and held up her hands. "Don't worry. I'll keep my hands to myself."

"Do whatever you want. He's a workaholic just like my dad and Conrad. He came downstairs this morning in a suit and tie and asked to set up his laptop in the dining room. He's been sitting there ever since. There's no way I'd ever get involved with a guy like him."

Chloe grimaced. "He put on a suit and tie to work remotely from your dining room?"

"Yes! That's what I'm saying! Workaholic with a capital *W*." She took another sip of her water. "Oh, and he does 'high-intensity weight training,' just like Conrad." She rolled her eyes.

Chloe laughed. "Well, that does it, then! Weight training? He's completely off the table."

"So off the table."

Chloe sighed. "'Yankee Doodle,' though. That's kind of endearing."

Laura smirked. "And Ted Bundy just seemed like such a nice young man."

They both burst out laughing.

Chapter Three

Jonathan looked up from his computer when Laura breezed into the dining room after lunch. She looked relaxed and happy in jeans and a purple cashmere sweater, and she smelled like citrus and coconuts. He felt stupid about it, like an unsophisticated schoolboy, but he found the scent delightful.

"Got time to talk about those documents now?" he asked.

She shook her head. "No, I don't, sorry." She sat next to him, took out her laptop and set it up on the table. As it was booting up, she turned and caught him staring. "Am I disturbing you?"

He gave his head a quick shake. "It's your inn."

She watched her computer screen for a second, then turned back to him and gave him an assessing look. "You have a video conference or something?"

"No. Why do you ask?"

"What's with the suit?"

He looked down at himself. Before she'd reappeared, he'd taken off his suit jacket and hung it over the back of his chair, loosened his tie and rolled his shirtsleeves up to his elbows, although he supposed he still looked pretty formal to someone like her, who seemed to live in jeans. "Oh. I think better when I'm wearing it. Puts me in the right mind-set for work."

She nodded and focused on her screen. He glanced at her screen, too. It looked like she was coding something in HTML. "What are you working on?" he asked.

"Building a website for my friend Chloe's restaurant."

"You're a web designer?"

She shook her head. "Hardly. But I've picked up a few things here and there. I'm hoping to make a little extra money to pay for some repairs on the inn."

"The roof?" he asked.

"How'd you know?"

"The water mark on the ceiling in my room."

Laura groaned. "Another one? Great."

"Sorry to be the bearer of bad news," he said.

She sighed. "I knew things were bad already. I just need a little more time to get my ducks in a row."

"After the sale, you won't need to worry about any of it. You'll be rolling in dough."

She rolled her eyes. "Yeah, because that's what *everyone* cares about."

He spread his hands. "Hey, there are plenty of people out there who'd be happy to have a little cushion."

"And you know *all* about living paycheck to paycheck, right, Mr. BMW?"

He was irritated by her assumptions about him again. He'd worked hard to get where he was today. He'd hustled for handyman work as a high school and college kid to pay for his room, board and textbooks at SUNY Albany. Then he'd taken a couple of years off between college and law school, living at home and working on his uncle's construction crew to save enough money to get through Harvard Law without racking up an obscene amount of debt. "I didn't grow up with money, you know."

She arched an eyebrow. "No?"

"No."

She studied him for a second. "Well, I did. And it's not everything it's cracked up to be."

They both turned their attention to their computers, but it wasn't long before he found himself trying to engage her in conversation again. "So, did you study computer science in school?"

"I was more interested in English and journalism back then. But I didn't finish college."

That caught Jonathan off guard. The thought of not finishing college was almost inconceivable to him, given what it had symbolized in his life: a ticket away from both his father and all the kids who'd bullied him because of the rumors about his dad.

"You didn't finish college?" he repeated incredulously. "Why not?" He saw a flash of defiance fly across her face and immediately regretted his tone.

"You have noticed the little person who trails around after me, right? Small, brown hair, likes to sing 'Yankee Doodle.'"

He grinned. "Yes, she's hard to miss."

"Well, I got married, then left school when I got pregnant."

"You must have been really young."

She crossed her arms warily over her chest. "I was twenty."

"Young," he repeated. "How come you didn't go back after she was born?"

"Hard to go back to school in Boston when you live on Cape Cod." She still looked guarded.

"Where'd you go?" he asked.

"Boston University."

"You could have transferred," he said.

"Yes, because I had tons of free time in between caring for my newborn baby, my grandmother and the inn. Plus dealing with the divorce."

He winced. "I'm not trying to criticize. Just trying to understand."

Laura sighed. "When you figure it out, let me know, okay? Because I've been trying to understand what happened for years now, and I still can't get my head around it."

He tried to go back to his own work, but he couldn't focus. "Your ex. He's not very involved?"

"More like he's not involved *at all*. He hasn't even met Emma in person, you know."

"What?" He felt something hot and fierce tear through him, outraged on her behalf. "How is that even possible?"

She shrugged. "He cheated on me with one of his law firm partners while we were still married. She got transferred to the West Coast before Emma was born and—poof—he was gone."

Jonathan scraped a hand down his face. "You're better off without him. You know that, right?"

Her lips quirked up, almost as though she was trying not to laugh at him. "I know."

Something uncomfortable occurred to him. "He was a lawyer?"

"I was wondering if you'd catch that." There was more of that secret amusement in her eyes.

"What kind of lawyer?" He was suddenly very worried that he knew this guy.

She laughed, but it sounded flat. "Divorce lawyer."

He scrubbed a hand over his face again. This just got worse and worse. "Please tell me he pays you child support."

"He does," Laura said slowly. "I don't use any of it, though. I put it all in Emma's college fund."

"Alimony?"

She shook her head. "We were married for less than a year."

"But you left school for this guy," he protested.

"I left school for *my daughter*," she corrected him vehemently.

He nodded. "Where'd he go to law school?"

"Boston University."

He felt some relief that it wasn't Harvard, but pressed on anyway. "Name?"

She lifted an eyebrow. "Does it matter?"

"I want to make sure I don't know him."

She touched the back of his hand, and he sucked in a breath at the unexpected contact, feeling like a schoolboy again. Since when did the casual touch of a woman's hand affect him like that? It was odd, and a little bit thrilling, all at the same time.

"I don't think you know him," Laura said. "You've

got Ivy League written all over you. You probably went to Harvard or Princeton or Yale, right?"

He nodded. "Harvard."

"See? You'd never slum it with some awful divorce lawyer from BU."

She was definitely laughing at him now, and he should be annoyed at her assumption that he was a snob, but he found he couldn't let this go. "He's giving all lawyers a bad name."

She smiled, and this time it looked genuine. "Then make it up to me. Show me you're not all the unethical, morally bankrupt people I think you are."

"All right." He held out his hand so they could shake on it. "Challenge accepted."

She laughed. "For real?"

"For real," he repeated, waggling his hand.

She put her hand in his and shook it. "Okay, Harvard. Enlighten me."

He pulled her to her feet and started walking toward the kitchen, still tugging at her hand. "Where are you taking me?" she asked, laughing and trying to dig in her heels.

"Let's go take a look at that dishwasher of yours."

Laura and Jonathan pulled up to the hardware store in Jonathan's BMW. She'd made a big show out of putting a towel down on the passenger seat so she wouldn't scuff up the leather. He'd rolled his eyes, but he'd let her poke fun at him. He wasn't nearly as uptight as Conrad had been.

Before they'd left for the store, he'd actually done a fairly thorough assessment of the problem with the dishwasher. He'd removed the air gap and discovered a clog in the drain tube. He'd tried to flush it out with water, but had quickly come to the conclusion that he needed a special brush. Hence the trip to Prime Eight Hardware, a mom-and-pop shop in a plaza on Route 28A on the way out of town.

The bell over the door jangled as they made their way inside. The store was small but packed with tools. If you ever needed anything that wasn't in stock, Jason or Angela Cline would special-order it for you so that it arrived the next day.

Angela looked up from the magazine she was reading behind the counter. "Laura!" she exclaimed happily. "Haven't seen you in ages!"

Laura grinned, going over and giving her friend a one-armed hug across the counter. "Not in at least five days, right, Ang?" Angie had six young children and claimed the only time she got peace and quiet was when she was working—alone—at the store.

"Where's Emma?" Angie asked, looking around as though she'd simply missed seeing the little girl.

"Girls' afternoon with Chloe."

Angie sighed. "What I wouldn't give for a girls' afternoon…" All six of Angie's children were rough-and-tumble boys—the youngest of them in the same preschool class as Emma. She lowered her voice and goggled her eyes at Jonathan, who was currently scouring the plumbing aisle. "Who's your friend?"

"A lawyer who wants to buy the inn for Carberry Hotels."

Angie's face fell. "You're kidding. You're selling?"

Laura shook her head. "My mom wants to, but I'm

going to do my best to convince her to keep it in the family."

Angie exhaled in relief. "I still can't believe Dot left the inn to your mom."

"*Half* the inn to my mom."

"Still. I mean, you were there with her every step of the way for the last five years. Who helped your grandmother redecorate the front parlor? Who helped her with all her hiring decisions? Who helped her with the accounting, the taxes, the publicity? Because it certainly wasn't your mother."

Laura shrugged. "I don't get it, either, but what's done is done. At least with Jonathan here, I know my mom's not going to run back to Hong Kong before we can meet the terms of the will."

Angie gave her a sympathetic look. "You think she's really going to last the whole summer here in Wychmere Bay?"

"To be honest," Laura said, "when she walked out of the meeting with the executor of the estate, I wasn't sure she'd ever set foot in the inn again. She's in Boston right now."

Jonathan walked up to the counter, brush in hand.

"You find what you were looking for, sugar?" Angie asked, playing up a very transparent, very fake Southern accent.

"Sure did," he said, taking out his wallet to pay for the brush.

"Hang on a second," Laura said, turning to the aisles. "There's something I need, too." She located the mousetraps and grabbed a big cellophane bag full of them.

Jonathan looked at her and raised an eyebrow. "You've got mice?"

"I think so. I saw some droppings in the basement."

"If they were big enough for you to notice, it's probably a rat."

"A rat!" Laura and Angie shrieked in unison.

"Calm down, ladies." He plucked the mousetraps out of Laura's hand. "I'll handle it."

Angie sighed and murmured, "My hero," as he walked over to examine the various rattraps on offer.

Laura swatted her on the arm. "Don't. He'll hear you."

Angie grinned. "He should be hearing *you* get all swoony."

"Don't be weird," Laura muttered.

Jonathan brought the rattraps up to the counter. Laura looked at them with trepidation. "Are those for rats or small dogs?"

"Can Emma get into the basement?" he asked.

She shook her head. "The stairs are steep. I keep the door locked."

He nodded. "Good. I don't want her to get hurt." He handed the traps to Angie, and Laura took out her wallet. He gave her a look that was almost offended and said, "Put that away."

As Angie rang him up, she chirped, "If y'all have some time before Emma's due home, you should go next door for the early-bird special. Two appetizers for the price of one!"

"Thanks, Ang." Laura gave her friend another hug.

They walked outside and Jonathan studied the

neighboring restaurant. "'Mr. G's Diner,'" he said, reading the sign. "What do they serve?"

"Irish-Indian fusion."

He gaped at her. He looked…different this evening. He still wore his dress shirt, but no jacket and no tie. He'd left the top button open at his neck, and he looked less in control, somehow, less "master of the universe," but also more relaxed. More free.

He was holding the bag with the dishwasher brush and the rattraps in his left hand. She had to admit that there *was* something kind of swoon-worthy about a man who knew how to take apart a dishwasher, and who wasn't afraid to wrestle rats.

"That's not a real thing, is it?" he asked. "Irish-Indian fusion?"

"Oh, yeah, it's real. And pretty decent, actually." Now that they were talking about food, Laura realized she was hungry.

"What's on the menu? Curry meat loaf? Corned beef tikka masala?"

"Uh, no," she said. "But come on. I can tell you want to try it."

He made a face. "Is it wrong that I'm scared?"

She laughed. "Yes, Harvard. Man up. A little experimental cuisine won't kill you."

"Are you insulting my masculinity now?" he asked, lips twitching. He was clearly more amused than annoyed.

She gave him a friendly little pat on the arm. "There, there, Harvard. Your masculinity is fine."

He snorted. "Just what every man wants to hear from a beautiful woman."

She felt a dip in her stomach. He thought she was beautiful?

But he'd already moved on. "I'm usually more of a burger-and-fries type of guy. You're sure you don't need to rush home for Emma?" He was clearly hoping for a last-minute reprieve.

Laura shook her head. "Chloe would adopt that child if I'd let her. They'll be out until bedtime, at least." She gestured toward Mr. G's. "Come on. I'll even pay, since you're fixing my dishwasher and doing my rat wrangling."

"No way," he said, opening the door to the restaurant so she could walk inside. "That's part of our 'prove lawyers aren't morally bankrupt' challenge. There's no quid pro quo."

The decor at Mr. G's was…interesting. Neither Irish nor Indian, but new age, with a rainbow string of crystal beads separating the kitchen from the dining room, star maps on the ceiling and miniature lava lamps on the tables throwing off an ever-shifting, colorful glow.

Jonathan waved his hand at all the weirdness surrounding them and, in a voice pitched for her ears only, said, "I don't understand what's happening here."

"Children, children, children," a plump blonde woman in her fifties—Colleen Gadepali, Mrs. G herself—came through the rainbow bead curtain to greet them, folding her hands and bowing low. She was wearing an elaborate green sari, and she had a distinct Irish brogue. "*Namaste.* Welcome to Mr. G's."

"Hi, Colleen," Laura said brightly, letting the older woman air-kiss her cheeks and then introducing her to Jonathan as Mrs. G. "How are you?"

"Happy days, dear. Happy days. Table for two?"

"Yes, please."

Only one of the other tables was occupied, but it was still on the early side for dinner. Colleen seated them and handed them their menus. "Can I get you something to drink?"

"Water, please," Laura said, while Jonathan asked for iced tea.

Once Colleen was out of earshot, Jonathan cocked his head to the side. "*Namaste?* Isn't that a yoga thing?"

"Yoga was invented in India, you know," Laura informed him.

"Really?"

"Never tried it, have you?"

He shrugged and opened his menu. "A bunch of weird stretches in a group exercise class? Nope." He scanned the menu. "Hey, this looks more like Irish *and* Indian, not Irish-Indian fusion."

She smiled at him, all innocence. "Does it? Well, there you go."

He turned his attention back to the menu. "What's good here?"

"The sausage and spinach skillet lasagna is fantastic. So's the shepherd's pie. Oh, and the eggplant gratin, and the chickpea curry, and the German onion pie."

He arched an eyebrow. "Hungry, are we?"

She smirked. "It's been a long time since lunch for me."

"Want to order a bunch of stuff and share it?"

She sat back, feeling irrationally pleased by his suggestion. "Sure." She was definitely hungry, and it would be fun to see what he thought of all the different food.

Colleen brought their drinks to the table. "*Sláinte*, children. Cheers." She bowed low to them again.

They ordered. When Colleen heard how much food they were getting, she moved them to a bigger table so there would be room for all the plates.

Jonathan watched the older woman walk off in her sari. "So, how did Mrs. G come to run an Irish-Indian restaurant?"

Laura laughed. "Mr. G has Indian heritage. And happens to be a great chef."

The food arrived and Jonathan took a forkful of the eggplant gratin without waiting for an extra plate. "Wow," he said, fanning his mouth to cool it down. The food was steaming hot and very aromatic. The scent of cheese and curry, meat and spice filled the air. "That's incredible."

"And to think you didn't even want to come in here," Laura teased, accepting two extra plates from Colleen they could use to portion out the food.

He grinned at her. "I may have been misled."

When they finished eating, he leaned back and patted his stomach. "So...dessert?"

"You can't still be hungry," she protested.

"Maybe a little walk first to digest?"

She drummed her fingers together. "Hmm, so Harvard has a sweet tooth, does he?"

"My one vice. Don't tell anyone."

She laughed. "Your secret's safe with me."

He paid for dinner and they left the restaurant. Outside, he glanced down the street. "Which way?"

She turned to the left. "Follow me. There's a candy store I think you'll like."

"Sold," he said, walking next to her. He studied the buildings they passed curiously—a mix of homes and businesses: a hair salon, a restaurant, a bank. They all had big yards surrounding them, although the lawns got smaller as they got closer to the center of town.

"How come all the buildings here are cedar shingled?" he asked.

She shrugged. "Just the style, I guess. Some of them have vinyl siding."

"Not many." He looked at another cedar-shingled house. "It's nice, though. Cohesive. You'll always know you're on Cape Cod."

A few minutes later, they stopped in front of a two-story building with red vinyl siding, a covered porch and flower boxes in the three windows upstairs. "The Candy Shack," Jonathan said, rubbing his hands together in anticipation.

"The Candy Shack," Laura confirmed with a smile. "Can't wait."

They went in. The walls were lined with penny candy bins full of peppermints and jujubes, licorice allsorts and saltwater taffy, bridge mixture and lollipop twists. The shelves were stacked with every kind of packaged candy known to man, including many international chocolate bars like Aero and Flake and Coffee Crisp. A huge glass display case housed rows and rows of homemade fudge.

Irene Perkins, her late grandmother's best friend, was behind the counter. "Laura, sweetheart," she said, adjusting her red-framed glasses, fluffing her short white perm and opening her arms for a hug. "Come here!"

"Hi, Irene," Laura replied, obliging the older woman with a hug. "This is Jonathan. He's here on business, staying at the inn for a few days."

"Hello, young man. I heard about you from my little roommate, Chloe." Laura always found it hilarious that *her* best friend lived in the apartment above The Candy Shack with her *grandmother's* best friend, but Chloe had been devastated when her parents were killed in a car accident, and having Irene on hand as her grandmother by proxy seemed to suit her just fine.

"Hello. Nice to meet you," Jonathan said, shaking Irene's hand. "Is this your place?"

"Forty-three years and counting," Irene confirmed. "Just like Dot and the inn."

Laura's grandparents had bought The Sea Glass Inn in the late '70s and run it together until her grandfather passed away when Laura was ten.

"Good for you," Jonathan said. "Looks like you do good business." He nodded toward the other people milling around the store.

"We do, young man. We do."

He leaned on the counter and gave Irene one of his easy smiles. "What do you recommend?"

"The fudge," Laura and Irene said at the same time. "Definitely the fudge," Laura added with a nod.

He laughed. "Fudge it is." He looked to Laura. "What do you like best?"

"Oh, my gosh, how can I choose? It's all so good. Especially the chocolate."

He ran his eyes over the labels in the case. "Choco-

late Almond, Chocolate Coconut, Chocolate Marsh-
mallow, Chocolate Peanut Butter, Chocolate Pineapple,
Chocolate Raisin, Chocolate Raspberry—" He broke
off and glanced at her. "Which one?"

She bit her lip. "I can't choose. They're all deli-
cious."

"You must have a favorite."

"Try the Chocolate Pineapple," Irene said. "It's our
newest recipe."

He looked to Laura, who gave a small nod. "Okay,"
he said. "Half a pound, please."

Irene smiled. "Good choice. I'll cut it into bite-size
pieces for you."

"Sounds great."

He paid for the fudge and followed Laura onto the
back patio, where there were a few small wrought iron
tables and chairs for customers to use. Beyond the
patio, there was a birdbath on the lawn and a veritable
plethora of garden gnomes in the flower beds.

Jonathan pulled out a chair for her. She wasn't sure
anyone had ever done that for her before. "Here." He
held out the box so she could select the first piece of
fudge.

Then he took a piece, popped it in his mouth and
groaned. "Wow. Chocolate and pineapple—who
knew?"

She tried her fudge and smiled. "Yeah, it's good."

"Good? It's phenomenal." He popped a second piece
in his mouth and then shoved the box in her direction.
"You have to take some more. Otherwise, I'm going
to eat it all."

She laughed and took another piece. "Now I know why you run every day, Harvard."

"You got me," he said. "I can't say no to chocolate." He sat back and enjoyed his fudge for a minute. "So, do you know everyone in town?"

She laughed again. "Pretty much. Especially the small business owners. Gram and I used to host Wychmere Bay's Small Business Association meetings every other month. Before she got sick."

"I'm sorry," he said. "Was it a long illness?"

She hitched a shoulder. She still felt raw about it, but she was determined not to cry. Gram had been her rock, her anchor—and now she was gone. "Emphysema. She had it as long as I knew her. It got worse in the last two years. Portable oxygen machine, the whole deal."

"I'm sorry," he said again.

"What about you?" she asked. "Are your grandparents still alive?"

"Just my maternal grandfather. He's ninety-four, still getting out for his walks, still living at home. It's amazing."

"Good for him. You see him often?"

He shook his head. "Not as often as I'd like."

"Why not?"

"He's in Upstate New York."

"And…?" She arched an eyebrow.

He spread his hands. "I'm always busy with work."

"That's too bad," she said. "I'm sure he misses you." She heard a seagull cry overhead and noticed that the light was changing. "Hey, what time is it?"

He checked his watch. "A little before seven."

"We should get back."

"All right," he said, standing. "Thanks for showing me around. This was fun."

She nodded. It *had* been fun—a lot of fun. "You have the bag from the hardware store?"

He held it up. "Right here."

"Okay," she said. "Let's go."

Chapter Four

When Jonathan was pulled out of bed by the sound of hysterical crying at eleven thirty that night, he worried that Emma had somehow gotten into the basement and set off one of the rattraps he'd placed after he and Laura had returned from their trip into town.

He threw on a shirt and poked his head into the hallway. It sounded like the crying was coming from downstairs.

He started down the creaky stairwell, and saw Laura pacing the length of the parlor in a long pink nightgown, a weeping Emma held tightly in her arms. "Shh, shh, shh," she crooned. "Shh, shh, shh."

"Everything okay?" he asked. He didn't see any blood, so that was good.

She stroked her daughter's hair. "Nightmare."

He came all the way down the stairs, touched the back of the little girl's shoulder. "You have a bad dream, Tiny?"

The girl sobbed harder, clinging to her mom.

"What can I do?" he asked.

"It's okay," Laura said. "She'll cry herself out eventually. You can go back to bed."

He looked at her steadily. "It's not like I'm going to be able to sleep."

She sighed and shifted Emma higher in her arms. "Sometimes we watch cartoons with no volume. Can you look for the remote, see if you can turn the TV on?"

He did a quick scan around the room and located it on one of the side tables. Squinting to read the buttons in the darkness, he figured out how to turn the television on. "What cartoon?"

She sat down heavily on the couch, Emma clutching her neck. "See if you can find some old Disney cartoons or something."

He navigated through the system, found some vintage animated shorts. He turned them on and hoped they would help.

After a few minutes, Emma quieted down, her sobs mellowing into hitching breaths.

"You like this one, Tiny? The one where Donald eats the corn on the cob like it's a typewriter?"

The girl looked at him, pushed a strand of tear-soaked hair out of her face and nodded.

"It's a good one," he said.

Laura eased Emma onto the sofa and caught Jonathan's eye above the girl's head. "Can you sit with her for a minute?"

He scooted closer to Emma and gave Laura a nod. "Of course."

The girl climbed onto his lap and laid her head on his chest and he froze, uncertain about what to do or where to put his hands. "You're not soft like my mommy," Emma murmured, and he relaxed a little, placing one arm along the back of the couch and the other around the little girl's back.

"Do you get bad dreams a lot?" he asked.

She nodded.

They watched the cartoon in silence for a moment. "Know what I do when I have bad dreams?"

She pointed her little face up at him. "You have bad dweams, too?"

"Everybody has them sometimes, Tiny. Part of life. But when I have a bad dream, I think about happy things. Like dancing," he said, thinking back to their conversation at breakfast, "or 'Yankee Doodle.'"

"I like dancing," she said sleepily. "I like 'Yankee Doodle.'"

"I know." He started humming the song for her, heard her sigh and then heard her breathing get more even.

Laura tiptoed back into the room, wearing a thick white bathrobe over her cotton nightgown. "Wow, you got her back to sleep?"

Jonathan looked down. "She must have just conked out," he whispered.

"It usually takes me like an *hour* to get her back to bed."

"Glad I could help. You want me to carry her upstairs?"

Laura shook her head. "She doesn't transfer well. We should wait until she falls into deep sleep."

"How can you tell?"

She sat next to him and Emma, and placed a hand

lightly on her daughter's back. "You've obviously never had to get a baby to sleep."

He felt his lips curl up. "Can't say I have."

"You've got to hold them for, like, half an hour. At first, they think they're still feeding, and their little mouths are moving, and they get these sweet little expressions on their faces, smiles and sadness and tiny quivering chins. But after a while, if you just keep holding them, their mouths relax and their faces stop twitching. Then you can stand up and place them in the crib and nothing will wake them. Their arms and legs will just dangle like dead weight. That's deep sleep."

He could picture her holding a sleeping baby, and the mental image gave him a peaceful feeling in his chest. What an idiot her ex-husband was, giving up these two for—what? A woman from his office who could boost his career?

"So, I hold her for half an hour, huh?"

Laura yawned. "Sorry, Harvard. If I'd known she'd fall asleep on you, I never would have left."

He let his head drift against the back of the couch. "There's a lot that falls on your shoulders, isn't there, when you've got a kid?"

She didn't answer, but she did let her head rest against the cushions, too.

"You ever get tired?" he asked.

"I'm tired now."

"She has nightmares a lot?"

Laura shrugged. "A few times a week."

"You can sleep. I'll hold her."

She yawned again. "Can't ask you to do that, Harvard."

"You didn't ask," he said easily. "I offered."

She turned her head to the side, burrowing a little into the cushions. "Well, if you really don't mind, maybe I'll just close my eyes for a second."

"I really don't mind," he said.

She closed her eyes. He watched the cartoon duck flicker across the screen and held a sleeping Emma until half an hour had passed and the girl was warm and loose-limbed in his arms. Standing carefully so as not to disturb Laura, he carried Emma to her bedroom and tucked her in. The little girl didn't stir.

He went back downstairs and turned off the TV. "Laura," he murmured, touching her shoulder. "Time to go to bed."

She groaned and tried to tunnel deeper into the couch, her hair mussed, her warm, soft skin giving off the faint scent of baby powder.

"Come on," he said, sitting next to her and sliding his arm around her waist. "I'll help you."

She leaned into him and they stood together, and he felt happy to have even this small opportunity to lend her some of his strength.

"Where's Emma?" she whispered, taking a step away from him, reminding him that she wasn't his to comfort, his to hold.

He pointed at the ceiling. "Upstairs. In bed."

She rubbed her eyes. "I must have been more tired than I thought."

He shrugged. "You've got a lot on your shoulders."

"Thanks for your help, Harvard. You definitely scored some points tonight."

"Points?"

"You know," she said, "the moral-bankruptcy thing."

"Oh, yeah. Right."

"Good night, Harvard."

He lifted his hand in a farewell wave. "Good night."

Then he watched her climb the stairs, feeling curiously disappointed that she'd been thinking of their challenge when all he'd been thinking about was...her.

When Jonathan walked into the dining room the next morning just after six, dressed in track pants, a T-shirt and sneakers, he was surprised to see Laura and Emma sitting calmly in a pool of sunlight at the end of one the communal tables. Laura was sipping coffee, and Emma was drawing a picture.

"You ladies are up early," he said.

"Mr. Jonafin!" Emma popped out of her seat and flung herself at his legs for a hug.

He laughed and picked her up. "Hey, Tiny. You get back to sleep after that nightmare?"

Laura shot him an apologetic glance and mouthed, "Sorry," over Emma's head. Jonathan ignored it. He didn't mind.

"I drawed you a picture."

"Oh, yeah?" He put the little girl down and she retrieved the drawing and presented it to him. It looked like a colorful maze. "Very nice."

"It's me at the beach! With the waves! And a mermaid! And a sparkly crab!"

"Wow, a sparkly crab, huh? That's cool."

"Do you want to me to sing 'Yankee Doodle'?"

"Honey, why don't we let Mr. Jonathan have a cup of coffee first?" Laura said.

"Okay. Would you like a cup of coffee, Mr. Jona-fin?"

"Sure, Tiny. That'd be nice."

She grabbed his hand and pulled him toward the sideboard, where there was a coffee machine, some creamer and a stack of mugs, along with some bread and cereal. "I had Cheerios for breakfast," she announced proudly.

"I'm partial to shredded wheat myself." He didn't reach for the cereal, though—just the coffee.

"Sweetened or unsweetened?" Laura asked.

"Unsweetened. With a protein shake. After my run."

"Ah, that's right," she said. "Your run. That explains the workout clothes. Sorry to say we don't keep protein powder on hand at the inn."

He grinned and pulled a travel packet of the stuff out of his pocket with a flourish. "That's okay. I brought my own."

She groaned. "Of course you did."

"What's a pwotein shake?" Emma asked.

"An adult drink, honey."

Emma scrunched her nose. "Yuck!"

Jonathan sipped his coffee. "Any good running trails around here?"

"Um, how about the beach?"

He ran a hand through his hair. "I wanted to save that for later. I like to be disciplined about my running, but I want to enjoy my first trip to the beach."

Laura squinted at him. "What do you mean, your first trip? You've never been to the beach?"

He shook his head. "Not here. This is my first time on Cape Cod."

She cocked her head. "Seriously?"

"Seriously."

"How long have you lived in Boston?" she asked.

"Almost ten years."

She gave him an odd look. "What took you so long?"

He shrugged. "I don't really take a lot of vacations."

"You don't have to take a vacation to come down to the Cape," she insisted. "Easy weekend trip from Boston."

"Maybe I'll come back someday," he said, knowing even as he said it that he'd never have time. But more and more, he found himself looking forward to seeing her and talking with her. And—boy!—was she ever good at making him laugh.

He'd like to see her again after this whole thing was over. But he knew better than to make promises he couldn't keep.

"Have you heard of backward day, Mr. Jonafin? On backward day, we have ice cream for breakfast!"

"Whoa, that's living on the edge, Tiny. What's your favorite flavor?"

The little girl's face scrunched up as she thought. "Tiger Tail Bubble Gum Fudge Sprinkles Banana Pop!"

"With whipped cream?" he asked. "And a cherry on top?"

"Lots and lots and *lots* of whipped cream! I love whipped cream soooo much!"

Laura ignored Emma's rapturous description of ice cream and told Jonathan, "I don't know about running trails, but there's a wooded path that cuts behind Main Street. I think you can follow it over to the next town. How far do you usually run?"

"Nine or ten miles."

She laughed. "Oh, yeah. Ten miles. A nice, leisurely jog. And weight training on the weekend, right? Don't tell me you're one of those paleo diet people, too."

He snorted. "Um, did you or did you not see me inhale close to a half a pound of fudge last night?"

"Could have been a cheat day."

He shook his head. "I don't cheat."

Her eyebrow shot up at that. "Ever?"

He looked at her steadily. He had the sense they weren't talking about food anymore, and it made him hate what her ex-husband had done to her all the more. "Never."

She bit her lip. "Good to know."

"Brianna cheats at Go Fish," Emma said. "And she cries when she loses."

"A cheater *and* a sore loser? Bad deal," he replied.

"Do you like Go Fish, Mr. Jonafin?"

"Sure, Tiny. How about when I get back from my run, we have a game?"

"Just a quick one, though, right, Em?" Laura looked at Jonathan. "She's got preschool this morning."

"After you drop her off, maybe we can look for those documents."

She gave him a sly smile. "I don't think so, Harvard. I'm taking you to the beach."

Chapter Five

Laura gestured toward the ragged line of boulders jutting into the sea, the small white lighthouse at the end beckoning ships to safe harbor. "You sure you want to do this?"

They'd both kicked off their shoes and socks in the cold sand at the end of the boardwalk. Jonathan had rolled up his pants, and Laura had done the same. They were surrounded by the pungent smell of salt-soaked seaweed, and aside from a woman in a wool hat walking her dog farther up the beach, they were alone.

"Of course I want to do this," he said.

"It can get precarious at high tide."

"Bring it." He made a beckoning gesture with his hands.

"Your suit'll get wet, Harvard."

He waved off her objection. "Small price to pay." He'd brought other clothes with him to Cape Cod, of course, but he'd put on the suit after his run knowing it would make her laugh to see him wearing it on the beach. And he found that the more time he spent with her, the more desperately he wanted to make her smile, see her eyes sparkle, make her laugh.

He took off his jacket and offered it to her. "Speaking of my suit, you look cold." She was wearing jeans and an emerald green sweater. Her cheeks were rosy.

She shook her head. "I'm okay."

"Really, take it," he insisted, settling the blazer on her shoulders. Engulfed in his jacket, she looked like a princess, her long hair unruly in the sea breeze.

She settled into the blazer, managing to look both awkward and grateful at the same time. "Thanks." They walked in silence for a moment, the jetty looming.

When they reached the start of it, she hopped lightly onto the rocks. "So, I never asked you. What kind of law do you practice? Real estate law?"

He shook his head. "Corporate law. Mergers, acquisitions, corporate governance, that kind of thing."

She was fleet-footed, practically skipping from rock to rock. Jonathan followed, a little less certain of the path but determined not to fall behind. The boulders were damp and sandy, dried barnacles peppering the sides. She stopped and looked at him over her shoulder. "And Carberry Hotels is one of your clients?"

She was beautiful. She was *so* beautiful. And underneath the teasing, sometimes tough-girl demeanor, she was sweet, too—sweeter than that pineapple fudge from last night. Everyone they'd run into during their excursion into town had loved her. He couldn't understand why men weren't lining up around the block to sweep her off her feet. If he had time for a girlfriend, he'd absolutely be the first person in line.

"Connor Carberry is my friend," he said. "This deal is like a test case. If it goes through, the whole hotel chain could become a client."

She cocked her head to the side, considering. "Interesting."

"So, what about you? When the sale goes through, will you go back to school? Learn web design or software coding?"

She waved her hand dismissively. "I don't want to talk about that right now."

They'd reached the end of the jetty, where there was a small unmanned lighthouse with a green light flashing from the cupola up top. A seagull dropped a crab on the rocks and swooped down to claim the meat from the shattered shell. Laura leaned back against the wall of the lighthouse, her hair wild around her face.

"What do you want to talk about?" he asked.

She gave him a teasing smile. "Tell me something about you no one else knows." He thought of their conversation from the day before: *show me lawyers aren't all the unethical, morally bankrupt people I think you are.*

A big wave broke over the end of the jetty, spraying their legs. "Whoa!" Jonathan gasped. The cold was bracing.

Laura laughed. "You wanna turn back?"

He shook his head. "Not a chance."

"Okay, Harvard. Something no one else knows."

He studied her for a moment, the way she was standing with her back against the lighthouse, his suit jacket hanging loosely from her shoulders, atop her windblown clothes. He'd never told anyone about his father before. Only his mother and his sister and whomever they'd chosen to confide in were aware of all that had happened.

"My dad has bipolar disorder. He was in and out of the hospital all through my childhood. He took off about fifteen years ago. We don't know where he is."

"Wow," she said, her mood instantly changing, all the playfulness fleeing her eyes. "That's—"

"Terrible? Yeah, I know." He gave a mirthless laugh. "It was right before I went to college. I almost didn't go."

"What made you change your mind?"

"Honestly? Fear. He wasn't diagnosed until his late twenties, after he'd already married and had kids. Which is actually really late for bipolar to manifest. But I figured if there was anything I really wanted to achieve, I'd better do it quick, just in case."

"And now?"

He gave her a wry smile. "And now I'm a lawyer. My dream come true."

"But no...?"

"Mental health issues?" He shook his head. "No."

"That must be a relief."

He shrugged. "I wish we could find him. I have resources now. I could help."

She leaned forward and squeezed his hand in sympathy. He looked up, startled, and had to fight the urge to pull her into his arms for an embrace.

He closed his eyes. Should he tell her about the private investigator's report? He didn't want to burden her, but he was tired of dealing with all of it by himself—of the nightmares that his father was ill and living on the streets somewhere, or that he'd given in to the depression that followed the mania and taken his own life.

"Have you ever heard of the Beacon Light Mission?"

"The one in Hyannis?" she asked. "Sure. I volunteer there every so often with my church."

"Really?" he said, his heart beating faster. He couldn't believe she'd been there. If the investigator was right, maybe she'd even seen his dad.

"Yeah, it's a homeless shelter. They hold chapel services every night and serve dinner to the homeless who attend. Emma and I go once a month with my Celebrate Recovery group to serve food and clean up the dining room after dinner. She loves it. She's always so happy to help people who are less fortunate than us."

Jonathan ran a hand through his hair. "I hired a private investigator a few months ago to see if he could trace my dad. The last lead he had was the Beacon Light Mission, from maybe six months ago."

Laura's green eyes got very big. "Are you serious? And you haven't seen him in fifteen years?"

Jonathan shook his head.

"Well, come on." She tugged at his hand and started back toward shore. "We have to go."

Laura could tell that Jonathan was nervous. For one thing, he hadn't argued at all when she'd insisted on driving to the mission in her beat-up Toyota Corolla instead of letting him drive them in his fancy BMW. For another, he'd hardly said a word the whole trip to

Hyannis, despite a constant stream of chatter from Emma in the back.

"So, what do we do when we get there?" he asked, opening and closing his fist, over and over, in his lap.

She glanced over and gave him a reassuring smile. They'd already been over this a couple of times, but she could tell that the repetition had a calming effect on him. He was obviously someone who liked discipline and structure, and she could imagine that being thrown so far out of his comfort zone was jarring.

"We'll check in with the folks in the kitchen, get our plastic gloves and then man our stations. They usually station Emma with the dinner rolls and put me next to her, serving soup or stew or veggies or whatever they've got on the menu that night. After everyone's been served, you're welcome to go sit with the patrons and see if anyone knows your dad."

"And the mission director—" he started.

"Dean," she supplied.

"Dean knows we're coming?"

She nodded. "I spoke with Pastor Nate this afternoon about it, and he called Dean and filled him in. He's cool with you asking people questions, although he did say that some of the people there might be unwilling to talk."

Jonathan blew out a deep breath. "Sure, that makes sense." Then he ran a hand through his hair. "This is going to sound terrible, but I was honestly shocked when the PI told me he might not be dead."

As she had on the jetty, she reached over and squeezed his hand.

He squeezed hers in return. "Thanks for coming with me."

She smiled, took her hand back and put it on the wheel. "Of course, Harvard. Least I could do after you caught that giant rat," she said, thinking about the rattrap he'd cleaned out earlier while she was on the phone with Pastor Nate.

"Rats eat cheese!" Emma piped up from the back seat.

"They do, Tiny. You're right," he said. "They like peanut butter, too."

"That's squirrels, Mr. Jonafin, not rats!"

"You're pretty smart, Tiny. Squirrels do like nuts." Then, turning to Laura, he said, "You might have more than one rat. I'm going to leave the traps set until I have to go back to Boston."

She nodded, but she had to admit she didn't like the thought of him leaving. Which was crazy. He was a workaholic lawyer who'd been here for only two days. So what if they had fun together? So what if he'd helped her out? So what if he got along with her daughter? A career-driven man was not the man for her. She didn't want to get involved with a man like her father, a man like Conrad, ever again.

She needed to remember that, then etch it into her brain.

Because when he was all nervous and vulnerable like he was right now, it made her want to let her guard down and take care of him. It was how she'd felt about Conrad when he'd get stressed out about his law school exams. Granted, searching for your long-lost father and worrying about getting a B on an exam weren't exactly in same ballpark, but the way she felt was similar enough to scare her.

She couldn't afford to let her guard down around Jonathan. She'd never be enough for a man like him—so smart, so ambitious, so successful. A man like him would only break her heart.

The mission was in an industrial part of Hyannis, the building a one-story concrete block with bars on the windows and a neon sign proclaiming Jesus Saves on the side.

She pulled to a stop in front of it. "Here we are," she said.

He rolled his shoulders, cracked his neck. "Wow. I feel sick."

"What's the worst thing that could happen?" she asked hypothetically. "No one will know anything, and you'll be in the exact same position you're in right now."

"You're right, you're right." He opened his door and got out. They went into the kitchen through a back door. Dean and a volunteer Laura didn't know were manning the ovens. The kitchen smelled like tomato soup.

"Hey," Dean said, turning to them. He was in cargo pants and a camouflage T-shirt. His hair always looked a little too long. "Good to see you, Laura, Emma. And you must be Jonathan." He held out his hand.

"I appreciate you letting me come by," Jonathan said, shaking Dean's hand. She was glad she'd talked Jonathan out of wearing a polo shirt tonight—he'd have looked *way* out of place.

"Any friend of Laura's is a friend of mine."

"It's okay to show people his picture?" Jonathan asked Dean.

"Sure, it's fine," Dean said. "Just, if anyone clams up or gets spooked, move on, okay? A lot of our people have this thing about authority figures. They might think you're with the cops or the FBI or something, and that could scare them away from getting the services they need."

Jonathan nodded. "Okay."

"Want to show me his picture?" Dean asked. "Maybe I've seen him around."

Jonathan fiddled with his phone for a second, then showed the screen to the other man. "This is an old photo, so I don't know if it'll be that much help."

Dean took Jonathan's cell out of his hand to look at the picture more closely. "Yeah, I don't know. Maybe. Hard to say. What's his name?" Laura took the phone from Dean so she could take a look. The man in the photo looked so normal. This whole thing was so sad.

"Dave. David Masters."

"Yeah, I don't know," Dean said again. "Plenty of Daves come through here, but we don't get a lot of last names."

"It's all right," Jonathan said. "It's a long shot, I know."

"Well, grab some gloves. We're going to start setting up the serving table."

"What's on the menu tonight?" Laura asked.

"Grilled cheese, tomato soup and salad," Dean said. "I think we'll put Emma on napkin duty, if that's okay with you, Mom?"

"Sounds good, doesn't it, Em?"

Emma did a pirouette in the middle of the kitchen. "I like grilled cheese."

"I know, honey."

The men carried big platters of food into the dining room and set them up on a long serving table. Emma took her position by the napkins, Jonathan held up a soup ladle and Laura got ready to dole out sandwich halves.

People started trickling in, and for the next half hour, the three of them served.

Jonathan watched Laura hand out another grilled cheese sandwich with a kind word and a smile. She was truly lovely. The fact that she and Emma came here every month just out of the goodness of their hearts was staggering. When was the last time he'd volunteered for anything more than another case at work?

He would never have come to a place like this if he hadn't been trying to find his dad, and the thought made him feel...small. Unworthy and ashamed. Because, when the lights were off and no one was looking, what kind of person was he? One who'd put work before everything else—his family, his faith, his community, his friends.

He still vividly remembered his first day as an associate at Meyers, Suben & Roe, how Mike Roe had given the associates his rules: no personal photos on your desk and no garlic in your lunch. He remembered how one woman had laughed behind Mike's back at how blatantly ridiculous those rules were and proceeded to place a framed photo of her dog next to her computer monitor. She'd been gone the next day.

The message had been crystal clear to Jonathan: if you weren't willing to put work first, there were a thousand other hungry young lawyers waiting for the chance to take your place.

He'd always thought that once he reached the holy grail of partnership, then his real life could begin. The life where he'd let himself have a relationship, maybe get married and have kids. But what if he didn't make partner? What would he do then?

He looked at the people around him in the mission, at their dirty hands, their unwashed hair, their giant backpacks and their multilayered clothes. He was pretty sure that these people had all had dreams once, too. How was it that some people's lives went so smoothly, and some people's went so far off the rails?

He wasn't going to let his life go sideways. He wouldn't. He couldn't. He had to make partner. He had to reach his goals.

A blonde woman with a sun-creased face and a handful of missing teeth approached him. He filled another bowl of soup and started to hand it to her, but she said, "I've already eaten, sonny. Come show me this picture of your friend Dave that Dean's been yammering about."

Jonathan looked to Laura, who smiled encouragingly. "The rush is over. I'll handle any soup requests that come through."

He followed the homeless woman to her table. He took out the picture of his dad.

Chapter Six

Jonathan woke up early to eat a quick breakfast before heading back to Hyannis. Things at the Beacon Light Mission hadn't exactly ended well the night before. A few people had thought they recognized Jonathan's dad, but no one had claimed any knowledge of his father's current whereabouts, and his questions *had* triggered someone's paranoia. The man had yelled, spit and tried to punch Jonathan in the face.

Dean had swooped in and de-escalated the situation quickly, then escorted Jonathan, Laura and Emma out the back door. "Why don't you come back in the morning? Say, seven o'clock. I'll take you over to the Salvation Army. They serve breakfast there, and a bunch of the people who sleep in the camps show up for it."

"The camps?" Jonathan had asked.

"A lot of the people who can't get into a shelter—or don't want to—end up in these makeshift tent camps in the woods."

Jonathan had nodded and told Dean he'd be back in the morning, first thing.

As he finished his bowl of shredded wheat, Laura came into the dining room, in jeans and a turtleneck sweater. She looked beautiful. He had to work hard to refrain from saying it out loud.

She sat next to him, touched his forearm. "You doing okay this morning? That was kind of intense last night."

He shrugged. "Not the first time someone's spit on me."

"Ugh, Harvard. Really?"

He hitched his shoulder again. "Kids can be cruel. I was picked on a lot in elementary school and junior high."

She gaped at him. "You were? Why?"

He gave her a sad smile. "You try having a father who has episodes like that guy last night and then ask me that question again."

"Oh, Harvard," she said, shaking her head. "And here I thought life with my dad was tough."

"What was your dad's deal?"

She waved her hand dismissively. "Typical rich kid problems. Low involvement, high expectations, super critical when we didn't measure up—which was, you know, pretty much always."

He blew out an audible breath. She'd said it matter-of-factly, but still, it had to have hurt. And he didn't like the idea of this woman being hurt by *anyone*. "Growing up stinks, doesn't it?"

She laughed. "Yeah, it kind of does."

He stood and picked up his bowl. "What are you and Emma up to today?"

"Playdate in the morning. In the afternoon, I'm not sure. Maybe just hanging out at the beach."

He smiled. "Sounds nice." He went into the kitchen and put his bowl in the dishwasher, which seemed to be working fine since he'd cleaned out the air gap. When he came back into the dining room, Laura was spreading peanut butter and jelly on a piece of toast. "Maybe later, we can get my documents together," he said.

She didn't look up from her toast. "Maybe."

"When's your mother getting back?" he asked, knowing that he'd for sure get access to the documents he needed *then*.

She gave him a look that was half helpless, half amused. "My mother's idea of roughing it is having to use the en suite hair dryer at the Ritz. The idea of being here at the same time as a rat would kill her. I don't know when she'll be back."

"No sign of any other rats yet," he said.

She crossed her fingers. "Here's hoping."

"I'd really like to get started on the document review before the weekend, if possible."

She gave a long-suffering sigh. "Okay, Harvard. When you get back, I'll see what I can do."

He drove to Hyannis. He met Dean. They went to the Salvation Army breakfast, which was a bust. No sign of his father there, and no one recognized the photo.

"Do you think it would be worth it for me to go check out those camps?" Jonathan asked as he and Dean headed back to Dean's car.

The mission director gave him a skeptical look. "Too dangerous. You'd get eaten alive."

"I can handle myself."

Dean shook his head. "Not there. Different set of rules. We're talking hard-core drugs and alcohol. Piles of rotting garbage, used syringes. People with knives and weapons. Some of the camps are even booby-trapped to stop outsiders from coming in. Trust me, you don't want to go there."

Jonathan ran a hand through his hair in frustration. He felt both so close, and so far, from finally finding his dad. "So, what now?"

"Text or email me his picture and I'll keep my ear to the ground, okay?"

Jonathan shook Dean's hand. "Thanks, man. Appreciate your help."

Dean dropped Jonathan off at his car, and Jonathan knew he should go back to the inn and round up that paperwork, but it felt like there was a vise around his chest—squeezing, squeezing. He didn't want to leave yet. Not when he was this close.

He should have done this years ago, when he'd first started making money, when he'd first started working at the law firm. The thought of his father being out here, on the streets, maybe in one of those camps, for the last six years while he'd been comfortably ensconced in his office was…horrifying.

His father had been out here on the streets and he'd hardly spared the man a second thought. He'd been busy and angry and detached. He'd had to be detached. After all the things his dad had put his family through, how could he not be?

But hard as he'd tried to wall himself off from those feelings, those memories, they were there, like a constant background hum, and right now they were pretty much all he could hear.

He needed a distraction, and work wasn't going to cut it. Not when he was here, and his father was so close. A duck boat drove by—like the ones he saw every day in the streets of Boston, but had never tried—and before he even really registered what he was doing, he'd dialed the landline at The Sea Glass Inn.

Laura picked up and he said, "Hey. It's Jonathan. Do you and Emma want to drive up to Hyannis and do a duck boat tour with me?"

When the girls arrived, Emma threw herself at his legs. "Hey, Tiny," he said, laughing and ruffling her hair. "You want to go in the funny boat?"

"Why's it called a duck boat?" she asked. She was wearing a ladybug headband with antennae, and her shoes were a sparkly red. "Does it quack?"

He pointed at one of the amphibious vehicles, open on the sides with a tarp on top. "It can drive on the road like a car but also float in the sea like a boat. So, it's kind of like a duck because of that."

"That's silly!" the little girl exclaimed. "Ducks don't drive!"

"Here," he said, handing her the gift he'd purchased at the toy store down the street. "This is for you."

"For meee?" she squealed, her ladybug antennae bouncing as she dumped the red kite out of the shopping bag and picked it up in her little hands. "Mommy, look! It's a kite! A birdie kite!"

"That's nice, honey. What do you say to Mr. Jonathan?"

"Thank you, Mr. Jonafin! Thank you so, so, so, so, so, so much!"

He laughed and ruffled her hair again. "You're welcome, Tiny. Maybe we can fly it on the beach later."

"Yeah!"

They got on the duck boat, which was only a quarter full, and the tour guide handed out duck whistles to all the kids. Emma happily started blowing. They drove through the streets of downtown Hyannis, which featured a large number of sights related to JFK—his church, his memorial, his museum.

The town, with its salty air and cedar shingles and oddball bakery that specialized in making treats for dogs, was similar to Wychmere Bay in its humility. There was no flash here, no ego. Just unpretentious people living their unpretentious lives.

When the boat dipped into the ocean for the wet part of the tour, Emma squealed in delight.

Laura touched Jonathan's wrist, and said in a low voice, "You didn't have to buy her a present, you know."

"I know, but I saw it in the window and thought she'd enjoy it, so…" He spread his hands. He hadn't flown a kite since he was a kid, and it had just seemed like it might be fun to take one to the beach and try it out.

"You sure you're doing okay, Harvard?" she asked softly. Her hair was getting windblown in the sea breeze.

"I'm just glad you two could come join me for this."

"I thought you needed to work this afternoon."

There was something watchful, something vigilant, in her eyes.

He shrugged. "I've literally wanted to go on a duck boat since I moved to Boston. Seemed too good of an opportunity to miss."

"And the stuff this morning?" she asked. "That was okay?"

He gave her a half smile. She was definitely perceptive. "It was okay. No one knew anything about my dad. But Dean was telling me about the homeless camps here. They sound pretty dire."

She gave his arm a little pat. From anyone else, it might have felt patronizing, but, from her, it felt... natural. Comforting. Nice. "Well, hopefully if he's still here, he's in a shelter. Or off the streets altogether!"

"Yes," he said, placing his hand on top of hers and pressing it to his arm for just a second before letting it go. "Hopefully."

He really did like her. He wondered if she liked him, too. Was she this kind and compassionate to everyone, or was there something special, in her eyes, about him?

Laura sat atop one of the dunes behind the inn, holding the red kite Jonathan and Emma had been flying before Angie and her boys showed up, the air cooling as afternoon turned into evening. Emma and Angie's four smaller boys—aged four, six, eight and ten—were trying to shoot Jonathan with Nerf guns.

He did a pretty good job of dancing away from the darts until the boys hatched a plan to tackle him. Then he had little guys hanging from his legs and his waist while Emma and the ten-year-old shot him with impunity.

Angie laughed and plopped down next to Laura as Jonathan went down on one knee in the sand, putting his hands over his face as the Nerf darts rained down. "Monsters!" She turned to Laura. "Does he babysit? Maybe he wants to take one or two of them home."

Laura smiled. "You birth 'em, you buy 'em, Ang."

Her friend drew her knees up to her chest. She was in her late thirties and had her auburn hair piled on top of her head. "How is this guy not taken already? Tall, good-looking, great with kids—I don't get it."

"You're seeing him in vacation mode. You haven't seen him in work mode yet."

Angie waved her hand. "Work, schmerk."

Laura watched him laugh as he pulled the Nerf gun out of the ten-year-old's hand and started firing. "For guys like that, work's all there is." She bit her lip as she said it, though, because she knew it wasn't true. She'd seen him at the shelter last night. She knew that work wasn't *all* there was to him, but it was a big enough part of who he was. It was big enough that she knew she had to stay away.

Angie gave her an assessing look. "You sound awfully cynical, Laura. It's not like you."

Laura shrugged. "Once bitten, twice shy, I guess."

"Well, *I* think he's great," Angie said decisively. "And now that Jason and I are expecting another baby…"

"Wait, whaaat?" Laura squealed.

"Yeah," Angie said happily. "It's a girl!"

"Oh, my gosh! Congratulations!" Laura threw her arms around her friend.

Angie returned the hug and grinned. "So, seriously, if he babysits, let him know I'm going to be in the market for a nanny pretty soon."

Chapter Seven

Laura took Emma out for breakfast every Saturday morning. Same time, same place, same pancakes. It was their tradition.

Without Emma, it was a five-minute walk from the inn to the restaurant on Main Street. With Emma, it was more like a twenty-minute walk, but that was part of the fun.

She led her daughter away from the beach, up Sand Street with its classic Cape Cod cottages and forested yards lined with budding oak trees and scraggly pitch pines. They saw a bunny and Emma tried to chase it, although it disappeared into the brush before she'd taken more than a delighted step in the startled animal's direction.

"Did you see him, Mommy? Did you see? He had a white tail like Peter Rabbit!"

"I saw him, honey. That was cool."

"Do you think Mr. Jonafin wants to see the bunny?"

"The bunny's gone now, Em."

"But he might come back, Mommy. Then Mr. Jona-fin could see!"

Laura bit her lip. She didn't know that he'd want to be bothered today. He hadn't done any work yesterday, and he might need to catch up. "We can ask him when we see him, okay, honey?"

"Okay," Emma said happily, already looking for the next natural wonder.

They ducked off the street onto a sand-strewn path that cut through a small wooded area, allowing them to bypass the gas station and the convenience store on the corner of Main Street and head straight to the more pedestrian-friendly section of Wychmere Bay's one-street "downtown."

As they rounded a bend, Jonathan came jogging toward them, face sweaty, color high. He slowed as Emma barreled toward him, screaming "Mr. Jonafin!" at the top of her lungs.

"Tiny!" He scooped her up and gave her a twirl, then set her down and wiped the sweat off his brow. "What are you girls doing out here?"

"We're going for breakfast, Mr. Jonafin, at The Barnacle Bakery! They have pancakes and meltaways and *everyfing.* You should come."

He laughed. "I'm not really dressed for breakfast, Tiny."

She scrunched up her little face. "You're dressed." She pointed at his running clothes. "Those aren't pajamas, are they, Mom?"

"Not pajamas," Laura confirmed. Her eyes flicked to his. "It's not fancy, I promise. Join us."

He held her gaze a beat longer, then smiled at

Emma. "All right, Tiny. I'll come, as long as you don't mind having breakfast with a sweaty runner."

"I can run really, really super fast!"

"How about super-*duper* fast?" he asked.

"Super-duper, *duper* fast!" Emma yelled, then demonstrated, running ahead with her arms held like chicken wings. They watched her in silence for a moment.

"Didn't mean to crash your parade." He knocked Laura's arm with his elbow.

"Did you see her face? You made her day."

He tilted his face to the sky. "What a morning. Even the air smells better here."

"Any good running trails connect to this path?" she asked.

"A few. Plenty to explore while I'm here."

"How long are you sticking around?"

He gave her an inscrutable look. "Until the contract's signed."

Emma ran back toward them, panting hard. "Was that fast, Mr. Jonafin?"

He ruffled her hair. "So fast."

"I'm *ti*-red," she whined.

"C'mere." He hoisted her onto his shoulders. She squealed and grabbed a handful of his hair. "Ooh, careful there, Tiny. That hurts."

She let go of his hair. "Sowwy," she said.

They came out of the woods into a parking lot behind a large white building with a clock tower. Once they were in front, he nodded up at the clock. "Roman numerals."

"Uh-huh," Laura said.

"Classy."

"This used to be a church. Now it's a second-run movie theater. But not one of those second-rate ones. This one has comfy couches and—what else, Em?"

"Ice cream!" Emma cheered.

Jonathan nodded. "Nice. I seem to remember that you like ice cream, right, Tiny?"

"Ice cream is yummy! Super-duper yummy!"

"Now, that's yummy," he said, mock serious, before giving Laura a little wink. If she hadn't thought he was handsome before, she certainly did now. "I saw a place down the street called The Sundae School. You been there, Tiny?"

"I *love* The Sundae School. I love it so much! It has the yummiest ice cream of all time!"

He laughed. "Of all time, huh?"

"Yeah! Yeah! Ice cream, ice cream, it's the best! It is better than the rest!" She was doing some kind of crazy arm calisthenics that were making it hard for her to balance on Jonathan's shoulders. He put her down, and she kept going.

He knocked Laura's arm again. "You've got a budding cheerleader here."

She laughed. "That's what I get for enrolling her in gymnastics."

They passed a string of storefronts under colorful awnings—a surf shop, a souvenir shop and a boutique clothing store with mannequins showing off the kind of clothes the Kennedys might wear: khakis, boat shoes and polo shirts, with sweaters tied jauntily around the shoulders.

She pointed at a three-story Victorian-style house that was painted a dark forest green. "That B&B across the street—the one with the wraparound porch that's set so far back from the road—is amazing. Very Victorian." She did her best imitation of a British accent. "They serve afternoon tea." She took Emma there every so often to partake of the finger sandwiches, biscuits and clotted cream.

They passed a bookstore that stocked only mysteries, a greasy-spoon diner and a souvenir shop with a fish-shaped weather vane on top. "They have weather cards in there that change color based on the level of humidity in the air. Emma loves them."

They passed an art gallery and a pizzeria whose main claim to fame was its old-school arcade games. "I still take a roll of quarters with me when I go to Franco's. Pac-Man, pinball—they're the best," she said.

"It's a real tourist town, isn't it?" Jonathan commented. He was holding Emma's hand.

"During the summer, sure. But during the off-season, everyone's pretty tight-knit."

Outside, they passed a sandwich shop and a jewelry store with pewter rings and gold-plated sand dollar earrings in the window before they reached The Barnacle Bakery, where they stopped to peer in the front window before heading inside.

"So this is it, huh? The famous Barnacle Bakery," Jonathan said. "What's a meltaway?"

"Kind of a cross between pound cake and a glazed doughnut. To. Die. For. The bakery line's always, like, ten people long, isn't it, Em?"

Her daughter nodded. "I like the pancakes the best."

"I like pancakes, too, Tiny. And eggs."

She squinted up at him. "Scrambled eggs? Or the gross runny ones?"

He held a hand to his heart, faked a stagger. "You wound me, Tiny. Scrambled, of course."

Emma smiled happily. "You're weird, Mr. Jonafin. But I like you anyway."

He ruffled her hair again. "You're weird, too, Tiny. We're a good pair."

They went in, got a table, placed their order. When the food came, Emma soaked her pancakes in strawberry syrup and then asked Jonathan to cut them up for her. He obliged.

"Do you have nieces and nephews?" Laura asked.

He shook some salt onto his eggs. "No."

"You're really good with them."

He shook his head. "Nah, it's just Emma. She's a champ."

Laura felt her chest puff up with pride, although at this moment her darling daughter literally had syrup *all* over her face. "Do you want kids?"

He looked up, brow arched. "Sure. Someday, maybe." He took a sip of orange juice. "What about you? Nieces and nephews?"

"My sisters are younger than me. Abby's only eighteen. She's at a finishing school in Europe right now. My other sister, Maddie, she's got some health issues. An eating disorder. Been in and out of hospitals and rehab centers for the last six years." After everything he'd told her about his father, she knew he'd understand.

He gave a low whistle. "I'm sorry. That's rough."

She sighed. "Yeah, it's hard. The best we can do is

support her, but you can't force someone into recovery. You probably know that more than anyone else."

"Still." Under the table, he toed her shin, similar to the elbow bumps he'd given her earlier. It was just a tap, a quick, reassuring touch, and yet… She wanted more. Despite everything she knew about lawyers and their ambition, she wanted more.

Her stupid, treacherous heart wanted more.

She blew out a breath, trying to let go of her childish desires, and gave him a shaky smile. "Still."

Emma looked up from the mess on her plate. "I want to go to the trampolines, Mommy! Mr. Jonafin, do you want to go to the trampolines with us?"

"Honey," Laura said, "I'm sure Mr. Jonathan has a lot of work to do today."

He put his hand on her wrist. She felt her heart rate kick up a notch. "Actually, this is kind of like a vacation for me. And it's Saturday. So, if you think I could clean up first, I could probably fit in the trampolines."

Emma jumped up and ran around their table in glee. "They're so much fun! So, so, *so* much fun!"

An hour later, after Jonathan had showered, shaved and changed into jeans, a dark blue golf shirt and a black windbreaker with gray fleece lining, they strapped Emma into her car seat and headed to the trampoline park. Now he smelled like aftershave—woodsy and fresh. Laura tightened her fingers on the steering wheel. She couldn't let her thoughts keep veering places they had no right to be. He was here on business. Period. And if he got what he wanted, she would lose the inn.

She stopped at the intersection of Sand Street and

Main, her left-turn signal blinking. "You're not wearing a suit today, Harvard."

"After all those sea stains the other day, I figured I'd better hang it up if I'm going to hang around with you."

She flicked a glance at him, a smile playing at the edge of her lips. "I warned you."

He nodded, his eyes dancing. "Yes, ma'am, you did."

They turned off Main onto South Street and passed a nine-hole golf course. "Mommy takes me golfing there, Mr. Jonafin! I'm weally good!"

"I believe it, Tiny!" Then, to Laura: "You golf?"

"I played with my dad growing up. It was pretty much the only time I saw him for more than ten or fifteen minutes at a time."

"Where was he the rest of the time?"

"He was a consultant at one of those big management consulting firms. He traveled a lot, worked long hours. For the past eleven years, he's headed up their office in Hong Kong."

"Ah."

Next to the golf course was a cemetery with old, moss-covered gravestones, many of them from the 1800s. Laura pointed. "Tip O'Neill and a few other famous people are buried there."

"'It's not where a man lands that marks his punishment. It's how far he falls,'" Jonathan droned in a deep, newscaster-style voice.

She gave him a skeptical glance. "Are you quoting Tip O'Neill right now? You're not that guy, are you? The quote guy?"

"'You can teach an old dog new tricks if the old dog wants to learn.'"

She laughed. "Oh, you *are* that guy! Harvard! Have you always been a nerd?"

He smiled and shrugged. He might even have been blushing a little. "I like US history. The more modern stuff, especially."

"Look, Mr. Jonafin! Look! The trampolines!"

They pulled into the parking lot for the trampolines, which were bordered on one side by batting cages and a go-kart track on the other. Across the street was a mini golf course, an A&W and a clam shack with pictures of lobster rolls and fried clams in the window. "Wow," Jonathan said, getting out of the car. "This is fantastic."

"Gotta keep the kids occupied."

Emma ran up to the chain-link fence surrounding the trampoline park, which comprised twelve outdoor in-ground trampolines. A few of them were already occupied, the kids twisting and twirling and doing splits in the air.

Laura went up to the cashier's kiosk to pay for Emma's admission, but Jonathan stopped her, wallet in hand. "Least I can do for forcing you to take me along."

Laura shook her head—if anyone had been forced to do anything, it had been him. Plus, he'd already paid for breakfast, but she had the sense he wouldn't take no for an answer. "Thanks."

They watched Emma leap onto her trampoline and start jumping. "She's got a lot of energy," he said.

Laura laughed. "You ain't seen nothing yet."

"So," he asked after a long moment, leaning back on the inside of the fence to watch Emma while she jumped, "did you go to high school in Hong Kong?"

"No, Boston. I was fourteen when my family moved. I stayed here."

"With your grandmother?"

She shrugged. "During the summer. I went to boarding school the rest of the time."

His eyes popped. "Boarding school? Wow. People still do that?"

"People still do that." Even to her own ears, her voice sounded flat.

She would never forget how her parents had left her with the headmistress at Chestnut Hill and taken off, not even bothering to see her dorm room or meet her roommate. Nor would she forget the stiff way the head-mistress had walked her over to the redbrick building that was to be her new home and said an awkward "Well, here you are, then" before going on with her day.

"I've always wanted to go to Hong Kong," Jona-than said.

"Yeah, it's something." She had mixed feelings about the Asian city. Hong Kong itself was vibrant and exciting, hard to forget even though she hadn't been back since Emma was born: the mountainous terrain with its steep, winding roads; the massive skyscrap-ers that lit up the sky with a laser light show every night; the harbor, the heartbeat of everything, letting the junks and ferries and cargo ships in and out.

But staying with her parents was always difficult. That feeling of forever trying—and failing—to live up to her father's expectations. That feeling that, some-how, if she did it—if she made him proud—maybe then she'd finally feel like she was somebody *she* could be proud of, too.

Coming to Christ had meant coming to terms with the fact that there was no achievement so big that it would ever fill the emptiness inside her. *God doesn't love us because we're so awesome and amazing*, she could remember her grandmother saying. *He loves us just because we are who we are.*

"What's your favorite thing about it?" Jonathan asked.

She thought for a moment, chewing her lip. "Re-pulse Bay Beach is beautiful. Very different from here. There's an open-air temple on one side, luxury skyscraper condominiums built into the slopes of the mountains behind it—one of them with a dragon hole right in the center of the building. You can swim al-most all year round. Lots of little jellyfish. They used to call it the Asian Riviera. It's gorgeous."

"What's a dragon hole?"

"It's a feng shui thing," she said. "They literally leave gaping holes in some of the buildings to let the dragons fly from the hills to the water."

"What? That's wild!"

She smiled. "Yeah, a lot of people think of Hong Kong as an Asian New York, but it's really different. I mean, yes, there's shopping, but it's a city built on mountains, so there's tons of nature, if you want to look for it."

"You like nature, huh?"

She gestured up at the sky. "Doesn't everyone?"

"Strong words for a city girl," he said.

"What? You grow up on a farm or something?"

He laughed. "Small town in Upstate New York."

"Moved away for college and never looked back?"

He hitched a shoulder. "Something like that."

"Would you?" she asked, watching Emma do sit-jumps on the trampoline.

"Would I what?"

"Ever go back to a small town?"

He cracked his neck. "Not a lot of job opportunities in a small town, especially for the type of work I do."

She gave him a measuring look. "And you like it? Handling mergers and acquisitions and contracts and whatever else you do in corporate law?"

"Contracts are important," he said mildly.

"Well, there you go, then."

"There you go."

Their eyes locked. She felt magnetized. He was everything she didn't want in a man, and yet... She couldn't look away.

He leaned in, his eyes dark and intense, and—

"Mommy! Did you see me? I did the splits! I really, truly did the splits! And I jumped *so high*!"

With a guilty jerk, Laura turned to her daughter and clapped delightedly. "Good job, baby! Good job!"

"Did you see, Mr. Jonafin?"

He gave her a big thumbs-up. "Nice work, Tiny! Show us again!"

Laura stood next to him, not looking at him, for the rest of Emma's allotted time on the trampoline, her mind churning. She'd never felt like this with her ex. She'd been flattered by his attention, thrilled that someone as smart and handsome and charming as Conrad wanted to be with her. But there had always been a certain element of *trying* with him. Of willing herself to be the person he wanted her to be.

There was an ease to spending time with Jonathan, a *comfortableness* she hadn't known before. When their eyes had locked, she'd felt... She didn't know what she'd felt, exactly, but it wasn't like anything she'd felt before.

It was then that she knew she was in real trouble.

The man had a big career that was important to him—more important than her, more important than Emma, more important than The Sea Glass Inn. He wanted kids "someday, maybe." And she'd known him for a grand total of all of four days.

She pulled away from him, crossing her arms over her chest. She might like Jonathan, she might think he was very attractive, but she couldn't let her feelings dictate her actions. She couldn't let her feelings for him carry her away.

Chapter Eight

The drive back to the inn had been…awkward. After their near kiss, Laura had seemed remote, almost cold, rebuffing his attempts at conversation with one- or two-word answers.

Jonathan had overstepped. He was sure of it. They'd been there with her *daughter*. He shouldn't have let himself get so carried away. He honestly didn't know what had come over him—it wasn't as though he didn't have self-control.

The truth was, the women he tended to date—casually, since he didn't have time for anything else—were all a certain type: career driven, status oriented, high-maintenance. Laura definitely didn't fit that mold. She was surprising. She was easy to talk to. She made him laugh.

And her little girl, Emma—he had no idea what to make of their instant connection. He didn't have much experience with kids, but that didn't seem to matter to Emma. She'd taken to him, and he'd taken to her right back.

You're losing your focus, man. He could practically hear Mike Roe's voice in his ear. *Forget about Laura and the girl and keep your eyes on the prize: The Sea Glass Inn.*

Ah, yes, the inn. His ticket to a partnership at the law firm...*if* the deal went through and Jonathan could convince the almighty Carberry Hotels to bring its business to Meyers, Suben & Roe. Even then, Jonathan thought ruefully, there was no guarantee that he'd end up as a partner. It suddenly seemed like an awful lot of effort for an outcome that was far from certain.

But what else could he do? He'd worked his whole life for this. He couldn't just give up now.

He looked out the window in his room—the view was nice, but only one window was usable; there was an air-conditioning unit in the other one, cutting off his sight line to the beach. There was no phone in the room, and the door unlocked with an actual key rather than a card. This place was, most definitely, due for an update.

It was a sizable property, and he'd already drawn up conditional offers on the neighboring homes. The new resort certainly wouldn't be on the same scale as any of the flagship Carberry Hotels, but it could do nicely as a boutique resort. Connor had painted him a fairly vivid picture of the plans, describing large, airy rooms, a yoga studio, a spa, a small gym and juice bar, and beachfront painting classes.

He might be able to convince Connor to preserve the parlor or at least its design and fixtures; with its plate glass windows and the battered treasure chest and the sea glass chandelier, it *was* charming. The small and serviceable bedrooms, though, needed to go.

At any rate, it looked as though what he'd hoped would be a quick, three- or four-day trip to do some initial due diligence, draft a contract and get it signed was going to turn into a full week here, maybe even two, what with Laura's reluctance to compile the documents he needed and the fact that Eleanor Lessoway was still MIA.

A week or two was fine, though. He could do his other work remotely, and it was definitely more relaxing to work from here than the office.

He took out his laptop. It might technically be the weekend, but truthfully, weekends never gave him much of a break. He got through the new emails in his inbox before he heard a tentative knock on his door.

"Mr. Jonafin?" Emma looked up at him with her big green eyes. "We've got pizza for dinner."

He crouched down to talk to her. "Thanks, Tiny. Your mom know you're inviting me?" Laura had been so cool toward him earlier—he hoped she'd started to thaw out.

"Mr. Brett and Aunt Chloe said to get you."

Mr. Brett? The stab of jealousy was as uncomfortable as it was unfamiliar. *Who was Mr. Brett?*

Downstairs, in the dining room, Chloe—the woman from the other night, the one with an obvious penchant for thrift store clothes—and a well-built guy with shaggy hair were standing at the sideboard, bickering over which pizza toppings were the best.

"Help me out here, man," the tall, shaggy-haired guy said with a nod of acknowledgment to Jonathan, waving a small piece of pineapple around. "There is no way fruit belongs on pizza."

Chloe swatted him with her empty paper plate. "Don't mess with my pineapple! We got you your meat lover's pizza. No need to mess with mine." She held out a plate to Jonathan. "What do you like? We've got meat lover's, Hawaiian, cheese and a couple of meatball grinders."

"Grinders?" he asked, not sure what they were.

"Subs," she replied.

"That sounds good."

Chloe plopped one on his plate. It was heavy. It smelled good. "And cheese for Ms. Emma," she said, laying a slice of pizza on a plate for the little girl.

Jonathan sat at the table and the other man plunked down beside him. "You must be Jonathan. I'm Brett."

"My oh-so-irritating brother," Chloe added, joining them at the table as the two men shook hands.

"All I said was that your shirt and your skirt don't match," Brett insisted.

Chloe sniffed. "Like you know anything about fashion."

Brett gave Jonathan an exaggerated eye roll and said in a low voice, "If that's fashion, then I'm the governor of Massachusetts."

Chloe glared. "I heard that!"

"You were supposed to!" Brett sang back brightly.

"I like your skirt, Aunt Chloe! The poodles are sooooo cute!" Emma gushed.

"Thanks, honey. You want to say the blessing?"

Emma obliged with a prayer Jonathan had never

heard before. "*A-B-C-D-E-F-G*, fank You, God, for feeding me. Amen."

"Amen," the adults chorused before digging into their dinners.

"Where's Laura?" Jonathan asked Brett as Chloe and Emma started a giggle-heavy conversation about noodle-eating poodles, tweetle beetles and a fox in socks.

"Had some errands to run. We told her we'd keep an eye on Emma—it's one of the last weekends we'll be available for a while."

"Oh, yeah?"

"Once the summer season starts in May," Brett said, "we're flat-out on the weekends at the restaurant."

"You own it?" Jonathan asked, remembering that Laura was building a website for them.

"Me and Chloe, yeah."

Jonathan nodded. "What kind of restaurant?"

"Seafood. The fancy kind. You know, 'haute cuisine.'" Brett put finger quotes around the French term.

"Nice."

"I wanted to sell it after our folks died, but Chloe wouldn't let me. Where else could a kid barely out of culinary school come in as the head chef?"

Jonathan winced. "Sorry to hear about your parents."

Brett waved him off. "All things work together for our good, right?"

Jonathan squinted, wary of platitudes. "Do they?" If God worked all things for good, why would his father have gone off the deep end? After all his hard work, why would he have to come down to Cape Cod to scrabble and scrap to make partner? Why couldn't everything just work the way it was supposed to— without all the hassle and heartache?

"You know it, man," Brett said easily. "Romans 8:28. Words to live by." He took a big bite of pizza, then hurried to chew and swallow. "Hey, you wouldn't happen to know anything about ball hockey, would you?"

Growing up in Upstate New York, hockey had been Jonathan's game. In the summer, the boys in his neighborhood had played ball hockey in the streets, pulling their goals to the side of the road whenever a car dared to drive by. In the winter, they'd flocked to the local park, where there was an outdoor ice rink that had never seen the underside of a Zamboni.

He'd play outside in the bitter cold for hours, sweating in his snowsuit, then come home and inhale the kind of dinners only a teenage boy could eat—heaping servings of meat loaf and mashed potatoes, whole boxes of spaghetti, entire chicken potpies.

Just thinking about it—the camaraderie, the physical exertion and the comfort of coming home to a well-cooked meal—made him nostalgic. How different his life was now: the sterile loft where he slept, the take-out meals he ate at his desk, the running he did by himself in the early-morning hours, before most people were even out of bed.

As much as he wanted to discount his childhood as unhappy due to his father's illness, he couldn't deny that there had been elements of it that had been wholesome and healthy and social—certainly a lot more social than the way he lived now.

"I know a little about hockey, yeah," he told Brett. "Why?"

"I'm doing this youth ministry thing. The kids want to play ball hockey, but I don't know much about the game."

Jonathan shook his head. "I don't know, man. I'm not going to be here that much longer—"

Brett waved his pizza in the air, and a piece of sausage fell off. "Doesn't have to be a big commitment. Come out with us tomorrow. You can be like our guest-starring coach."

"I'm not really active with church, let alone *ministry* work."

Brett snorted. "Dude, you say that like it's a dirty word."

"No," Jonathan insisted, "it's just, if you're looking for some kind of role model for the kids—"

"Man, I'm just looking for someone who can play the game. That's it."

"That's it?"

Brett nodded. "Yeah."

Jonathan thought about his experience the other night at the mission. Although it had been a bust in terms of getting a lead on his father, seeing Laura and Emma and the other volunteers giving back had been eye-opening. And the fact that he'd pitched in to help had felt…nice. "Okay."

"You're in?"

"I'm in."

"Awesome!" Brett gave him a fist bump. "One o'clock tomorrow afternoon. The parking lot behind the church. Be there."

* * *

Laura parked her car outside the inn and wandered down to Sand Street Beach. Outside the air was bracing, her breaths white puffs against the night sky. The sound of the waves hitting the shore filled her ears, and she kicked off her shoes and felt the cold sand worm its way between her toes. She loved the beach at night, the *vastness* of it, the stars sharp as needles over the deep gloam of the sea.

It was impossible to forget, out here, that you were just one tiny speck on God's great canvas. It was impossible to forget that, in the grand scheme of things, your problems amounted to little more than a fleck of dust.

She took in a deep breath and exhaled slowly, looking at the flashing light at the end of the jetty. She'd driven for an hour to get from the inn to Massachusetts National Cemetery in Bourne, where they'd laid her grandmother to rest next to her grandfather. The cemetery was *huge*, and even though she'd been there last week for the burial, she'd gotten lost looking for her grandparents' plot. Then she'd spent an hour by the graveside, a few minutes grabbing some fast food and another hour driving home.

She was lucky to have friends like Chloe and Brett—friends who understood what it was like to lose your mooring. Friends who were happy to step in, happy to help.

She thought about Jonathan and the way he'd swung Emma up onto his broad shoulders that morning, and how shaky he'd looked the other night before they'd gone into the mission to try to find his dad. She dug her feet into the sand. She wanted things she shouldn't want. She wanted things she couldn't have.

She turned toward the inn. Hopefully he'd still be holed up in his room, working or doing whatever it was he'd been doing since their near kiss at the trampolines.

Instead, she found him, Chloe and Brett in the parlor, watching a Bruins game on TV. Determined not to make things awkward, she addressed the room. "Emma asleep?"

"Yeah," Chloe said. "She was a perfect angel. We'll get out of your hair."

Laura put her hand on her friend's shoulder. "Stay. Watch the game."

"You sure?"

Laura nodded and sat next to Chloe. "What did you do tonight?"

"Ordered pizza," her friend said. "Then *Jonathan* over there insisted we take Emma out for ice cream."

"Of course he did," she replied. "The sweet tooth strikes again, huh, Harvard?"

He tore his gaze away from the game and held his hands up in mock surrender. "You're not one of those no-sugar moms, are you?"

Relieved that the awkwardness between them seemed to have dissipated, she shot back, "You saw how much syrup she put on her pancakes, didn't you?"

He grinned. "Okay, then. Good."

"She have fun?"

"Yummiest ice cream of all time," he said, his voice a little breathless. He managed to keep a straight face for about two milliseconds before he broke back into a grin.

Laura snorted. "You really are a nerd, aren't you?"

He patted his chest. "Oh, no! Forgot my pocket protector in Boston."

Chloe was looking back and forth between them, a bemused look in her eyes. "*Aaaand* that's our cue." She whacked Brett on the foot to get him up. "Good night, all. Peace out."

"Nice to meet you, man. See you tomorrow," Brett said to Jonathan, giving him a goodbye fist bump.

"One o'clock," Jonathan said.

Brett nodded. "You got it."

The door closed behind them, and Laura turned to Jonathan. "What's at one o'clock tomorrow?"

"Ball hockey."

"Oo-kay."

He shrugged. "Brett needs help with some youth ministry kids or something."

"Oh. Oh! That's nice of you to help."

He hitched his shoulder again. "I don't know how much help I'll be. I haven't played in a long time."

"Such modesty, Harvard." She gave his shin a playful kick. "I bet you were the captain of your fancy Ivy League team, weren't you?"

He laughed. "No. But I played all kinds of hockey growing up—ice hockey, field hockey, street hockey, you name it."

Now it was Laura's turn to laugh. "You'll be great. The kids will love you."

"Yeah?" There was something oddly vulnerable, oddly hopeful, in his eyes.

"If Emma's any indication…yeah, for sure."

"She's a sweet kid," he said. "You're obviously doing something right."

She always felt strange when people complimented her parenting, as though she was taking credit for something she hadn't earned. "Gram always said kids are their own little people right from the start. The hard work for a parent is to just not screw them up."

"Like I said," he reiterated, "you're clearly doing a great job."

She bit her lip, stared off into space. She didn't feel like she was doing such a stellar job of things, especially not lately, when she'd been so distracted by everything that had happened with Gram. But she couldn't tell him that, could she? After this morning, she knew she needed to keep her guard up around him. Needed to keep herself safe.

She could feel him watching her, though. Feel his gaze. She'd spent over an hour at her grandmother's graveside tonight. She was tired and lonely and sad. Regardless of whether or not it should be up, her guard was down.

After a long moment, he said, "Did I say something wrong?"

She shook her head, still biting her lip.

"Then, what?" he asked, looking genuinely concerned. "What is it?"

"It's just… Sometimes it was easier, before Gram got sick. To think that her dad's not being here wouldn't make such a big difference. That it wouldn't mess Emma up."

"Why would it have to mess her up?" he asked, his voice low.

She laughed, but there was no humor in her tone. "Well, my own dad was there but he wasn't *there*, not in the way that matters, and look at my sister. Look at me."

His eyes were puzzled. "What about you?"

She hitched a shoulder. "Married at twenty. Divorced at twenty-one. Wanting him to give me the love I never got from my father, but choosing the exact same kind of man."

He waved his hand dismissively. "That guy was a jerk."

"But I picked him, Jonathan. I said yes." That was the crux of it, right there—why she hadn't even tried dating since Conrad left. Because she couldn't trust herself. She had bad instincts when it came to men.

"People make mistakes," he said. "People learn."

She rubbed her face. "Sometimes I feel like I'm setting her up for failure."

He leaned forward and took her hand the way she'd taken his on the jetty, and in the car on the way to Beacon Light. "She's a beautiful, happy kid. The only thing you're setting her up for is *success*."

She bit her lip again, looked him in the eye. "You think?"

He nodded. "I *know*."

She let his confidence buoy her, and released a long breath. "Thanks."

He ran his thumb lightly over her knuckles before letting her hand drop. Then he sat back and crossed his ankle loosely over his knee. "Your friends are nice."

She nodded. "They're awesome."

"Think you can help me get those documents together tomorrow? I really need to get moving on the purchase offer. My boss is going to send out a search party for me if I don't get back to the office pretty soon."

Laura considered the man in front of her. He was wearing the same clothes he'd been wearing at the trampoline park, his blue golf shirt open at the collar, his dark hair unruly without its usual gel. It was late, and he had a definite five o'clock shadow going on.

She was fairly certain he had no idea about the stipulation her grandmother had made in her will. She thought about telling him about it then and there, but selfishly decided to keep her mouth shut. She didn't want him to leave just yet. Let him stay for the weekend, and then she'd give him all the documents, and then he'd go.

"Why is this deal so important to you?" she asked.

"I'm a sixth-year associate at my firm. It's now or never if I want to make partner."

"And without this deal, you don't think you're going to make it?"

He looked away. "Without this deal, I *know* I'm not going to make it. My boss told me as much last week."

"I'm sorry," she said.

His mouth quirked into a half grin. "It's weird. I had this plan, you know? From the time I was maybe twelve or thirteen, I always knew I was going to get a college scholarship, get into law school and work for one of the top-tier law firms. I didn't care that the hours would be crazy. I didn't care that I'd be on call day and night, vacations, holidays, dates, whenever—because in the end, there'd be this huge payoff. I'd be a partner. I'd be made." He stared at the wall. "Now... I don't know, it's like, if this thing doesn't happen, were the last twenty years of my life just a waste? Was it all for nothing?"

She recognized his pain—boy, did she ever. Before she'd found Christ, she'd done all the right things, checked all the right boxes, and still, when her parents had moved away and left her, all her self-esteem had gone up in smoke. For a couple of years, everything had felt so precarious—as though the rug could be pulled out from under her at any moment, as though the other shoe was always about to beat her over the head. It was an exhausting way to live, knowing you were building castles on sand but unaware that there were any other options.

"Nothing is for nothing," she said carefully. "Ultimately, all things work together for our good."

He raked a hand through his hair, which was all over the place. Laura had to tamp down an urge to reach up and smooth it down.

"You're the second person to quote that verse to me this evening."

Her eyebrow shot up. "Then maybe it's something you really needed to hear."

He raised a shoulder noncommittally. "Maybe."

"Do you, um... Do you want to go to church with us tomorrow? Me and Emma?" For some reason, her heart was pounding. She hadn't intended to invite him to worship with her—the invitation had just slipped out, almost as though her words were not her own.

Was this what God wanted from her? To witness to this man?

His eyes went wide. "I'm not really much of a churchgoer."

"I wasn't, either," she said simply, "until I was."

"I've got a lot of work to do tomorrow."

"I think you should come," she said quietly. "I...I'd like it if you came."

"You would?"

She nodded.

"Church, huh?" He scraped a hand across his jaw. "My mom would be happy. I guess I'll come."

Chapter Nine

Jonathan dressed in a suit and tie for the church service and headed downstairs in search of coffee. He wasn't disappointed. The dining room was filled with the scent of an aromatic hazelnut brew. "Hello?" he called out, peeking into the kitchen.

"Mr. Jonafin!" Emma shouted. She was helping her mom take the dishes out of the dishwasher, but jumped off her step stool at the sight of him to give him a hug.

He ruffled her hair. "Morning, Tiny." Then he turned to Laura. "Hey. Any problems with the dishwasher?"

She shook her head and smiled. "You did good, Harvard. Works like a charm."

He felt a jolt of satisfaction run through him. If he could have nothing else, he wanted to leave here knowing that he'd made this woman's life a little bit easier. "I'm glad. I'll check the rattraps in a minute."

"There's coffee in the dining room."

"Thanks," he said. "How about it, Tiny? Want to help me get my breakfast?"

"Yeah!" she cried, charging ahead.

Laura put the last plate away and wiped her hands on a dish towel. "If you don't go quickly, she's going to pour you a bowl of Lucky Charms, Frosted Flakes and Cap'n Crunch."

He rubbed his hands together like a greedy old man. "You know I love me some sugar."

Her eyes twinkled. "But not unless you get out for your run."

Ah, he thought wistfully, *she already knows me so well.*

"Can I ask you something?" he said.

She leaned against the kitchen counter. "Shoot."

"When was the last time this place was updated?"

"What?" She did a Vanna White flourish to indicate the very '70s kitchen around them. "You don't like retro?"

"Um, not when it's a PR term for 'old and run-down.'"

"Ouch."

"No offense," he said quickly.

She grinned. "None taken."

Emma popped back into the kitchen. "Mommy, I spilled the milk."

"Okay, honey, I'm coming." She grabbed a dishrag and followed Emma into the dining room. Jonathan trailed after them. Laura mopped up the milk and then looked at him. "You mind watching her for a few minutes while I get ready for church?"

"Of course not. What'd you make for me, Tiny?"

Sure enough, she'd poured him a bowlful of as-sorted sugar cereals, and also made him a piece of "yogurt toast." It wasn't the best thing he'd ever eaten, but it also wasn't the worst.

It didn't take Laura long to get ready, and before he knew it, he was walking toward a white clapboard church with a bell tower next to Laura and Emma, feeling completely out of place. The grass out front was sparse, the ground beneath it sandy. Seagulls swooped overhead.

He couldn't remember the last time he'd been to church—he hadn't gone home last Christmas, choosing instead to work and grab Chinese takeout with a couple of his colleagues from the firm. He'd rationalized it by saying his sister would be with his mom, but really, how far away was Upstate New York? A half day's drive from Boston, and he hadn't been able to find the time to see her on what was arguably the most important day of the year?

Up ahead Brett and Chloe stood by the doors to the church, smiling as they ushered people inside. Chloe was in a colorful, patterned '80s dress, complete with shoulder pads. Her brother Brett's hair was slicked back this morning, and he was wearing very respectable pressed gray pants and a collared shirt. "Jonathan," he called, holding out his hand. "Good to see you, man."

Jonathan nodded and clasped his hand. "Brett. Chloe."

Chloe shot a significant glance at her friend, then turned to him, beaming. "We didn't expect to see you here this fine morning."

He looked at Laura, who was blushing, and didn't know what to say. From inside the church, the first notes of a worship song started up. "Oh, better head in," Brett directed.

"Save us a seat?" Chloe asked Laura.

"Sure thing."

Laura dropped Emma off at her Sunday school class, and then led Jonathan up the center aisle of the church to a pew in the third row. He hung back as she slipped in and greeted a woman who slid down to make room for them.

In front of them, behind the altar, was a projection screen with the words to the song the band—featuring an electric keyboard, three guitars and drums—was playing. Beside him, Laura launched into the song wholeheartedly, a hymn about chains breaking, hearts changing, people being freed and forgiven.

After the song, people clapped boisterously from the pews. One of the guitarists, bespectacled and wearing dark blue jeans, set his instrument down and wandered to the pulpit.

"Isn't that what we all want?" the pastor/guitarist said mildly, removing his glasses to clean them on his blue linen shirt. "To be free? Free from sin? Free from death? Free from the ties that bind us?"

"Amen!" a couple of people called out. Jonathan shifted uncomfortably in his seat. He wasn't used to ardent worship. He wasn't used to *people* who were passionate about anything other than money and power and well-tailored suits.

From the aisle Chloe touched his shoulder, and Jonathan got up so she could sit on the opposite side of Laura. Brett sat next to him, on the end of the row.

"We're going to talk more about freedom a little

later in the service," the pastor went on, "but before we get started, I see some new faces here this morning. Let's take a moment to welcome them to Wychmere Community Church."

With that, the pastor strode out of the pulpit and straight to where Jonathan was sitting. "Hi. Pastor Nate Anderson. It's good to meet you." Jonathan felt his cheeks heat as he shook hands with the man.

After the service, in the church hall, Laura took a bite of her maple-frosted doughnut and looked toward the coffee machine, where Brett and Pastor Nate had cornered Jonathan.

"So, spill it, sister. What's the story?" Chloe steepled her fingers and gave her shoulder pads an anticipatory shake.

Laura suppressed a wry smile. "I don't know what you're talking about. There's no story."

"Oh, come on," Chloe said. "He obviously likes you. You two were getting seriously flirty last night."

"We were not!"

Chloe laughed. "You're hilarious."

Laura shook her head. "This is a business trip for him, that's all."

"It's business, sure. But he also likes you."

"I—" Laura stopped. "We don't have the same values. It would never work."

"What would it hurt to give the guy a chance?"

"And end up with someone like my dad or Conrad, who works sixteen hours a day? No, thanks."

Chloe took a bite of her Boston cream doughnut,

a splotch of cream falling onto her dress. "Not every guy with a good job is a snake like Conrad, you know."

"I know," Laura conceded, "but if I ever get married again, I want to be with someone who actually cares about being part of a church community and doing the right thing."

Chloe raised an eyebrow. "Who said anything about getting married?"

Laura felt her face heat up. She was *not* thinking about marrying Jonathan. That was beyond absurd, and she was mortified with her choice of words. To cover up her embarrassment, she made her next statement general and hypothetical. "Why date if you don't want to get married?"

"Um, I don't know, sister. Fun?"

Laura gave her a skeptical look. "I've got a daughter, Chlo. I'm not looking for fun." She paused for a split second—thinking of how much fun it was to talk to Jonathan, watch him play with Emma—and then added, "Or not *just* fun, I guess. I want forever, too."

"Fair enough," Chloe said, licking the last of her doughnut off her fingers. "But maybe if you stop waiting around for *forever, forever* will come to you." She glanced pointedly at the guys, and Laura followed her gaze. Surprisingly, Jonathan didn't look uncomfortable or out of place here in the church hall. He actually looked engaged with whatever Brett and Pastor Nate were saying.

"And isn't it *strange*," Chloe continued, slanting a coy glance at her friend, "that the man who doesn't know what to do with the fact that you're a Christian shows up here with you?"

Laura shrugged, trying not to get too wrapped up in what Chloe was trying to say. "I thought about what Gram always said about being a good witness."

"A good *witness*, huh?" Chloe grinned.

Laura gave her friend a quelling stare. "Yes, Chlo, a good witness."

"All righty, then. Here comes your man." She swirled her hand in a mock flourish. "Witness away."

Jonathan hadn't expected to like Pastor Nate. In fact, ever since the man had singled him out to shake his hand at the beginning of the service, Jonathan had been bracing himself for an onslaught of prayer and preaching.

But here in the church hall, eating doughnuts and drinking coffee, Nate hadn't been interested in talking about religion at all. He was way more interested in talking sports—specifically the Red Sox, the Patriots and the Bruins.

"Bruins game against the Leafs is coming up on Wednesday. Some of the guys are coming over to my place to watch," Nate said. "You in?"

Jonathan did a quick mental calculation and decided it was unlikely that he'd get everything for The Sea Glass Inn deal wrapped up by Wednesday. "I'll be there."

"Good deal." Brett punched him companionably on the arm.

"Well, it was great to meet you, Jonathan." Nate clasped his hand in farewell. "See you again soon."

Nate walked off to mingle with other parishioners, holding men's shoulders, kissing women's cheeks and smiling reassuringly at one and all. Jonathan squinted after him, an uneasy feeling in his gut.

Had he just been hoodwinked? Come watch a hockey game, then come to Jesus? Jonathan was a lawyer—he knew better than anyone that most things in life were about the quid pro quo. "Did he just do some spiritual brainwashing on me?" he wondered aloud.

Brett laughed. "What?"

"You know, is this how you guys recruit people? Invite them to some social event and then lure them back to church?"

Brett laughed again. "Dude, either you've got a very low opinion of preachers or a very low opinion of yourself. I promise you, nobody here's in the business of recruitment. All Nate was doing was trying to be friendly."

Jonathan took a swig of his coffee, which was luke-warm now and definitely not a gourmet blend. "That's pretty friendly, inviting someone you've just met over to your place."

"It's a playoffs party, man, not some master plan to initiate you into a cult."

"Still."

Brett shrugged. "I'd be happy to see you there, in-troduce you around."

When was the last time anyone had said they'd be happy to see him? He thought about his colleagues at the law firm, with whom he'd sometimes socialize after work—but that was more about proximity than any real camaraderie. He thought about the women he'd dated, who had been more interested in his wallet and career prospects than his companionship. He thought about his mother and his sister, neither of whom he'd made any effort to see in months and months.

What was wrong with him? Why were the only truly intimate relationships in his life the ones he went out of his way to avoid? And why did a small gesture of friendship set off all kinds of internal alarms? Since when had he become so cynical?

"I'd like to watch the game with you guys," he said quietly to Brett. "Sorry if I was being a jerk."

Brett hitched a shoulder. "I get it. You don't want to get roped into anything."

"Exactly," Jonathan said, feeling relieved that Brett understood.

Brett's gaze flicked to where Chloe and Laura were standing. "If you don't want to get roped into anything, it's probably best not to spend so much time with a certain single mom."

Jonathan felt his jaw tighten. "She's not like that."

Brett held up his hands. "Oh, I know *she's* not," he said quickly. "But I've seen guys who look at women the way you look at her, and if you're not planning to stick around, I'm worried it's going to end badly for *you*."

Jonathan's eyes flew to Laura. Was it really that obvious how much he liked her? Did he wear his heart on his sleeve?

"Do you think she'd ever move to Boston?"

Brett clapped a hand on his shoulder. "Brother, if you're already asking that question, you might be in deeper than you think."

Chapter Ten

Brett and Jonathan invited Emma to come to the ball hockey practice after lunch, so Laura found herself watching her daughter get fitted for a helmet, stick, shin guards and hockey gloves. Emma was definitely the youngest player, although all the kids were twelve and under, and there were a couple of boys who couldn't have been more than six years old. Jonathan spent a lot of time showing Emma how to hold her stick and hit her ball.

They did a bunch of drills: running with the ball, push passes, shooting on an empty net. At the very end of the practice, they scrimmaged for a few minutes, Brett serving as the captain of one team and Jonathan as the captain of the other.

Emma was sweaty and exhilarated when her team—Jonathan's team—won. The kids all knocked gloves with each other before taking off their gear.

"You did it, man." Brett gave Jonathan a fist bump as the last of the kids dispersed. "You spent an afternoon in ministry and you didn't run for the hills."

Jonathan laughed and turned to Emma. "What do you say, Tiny? Does this call for a celebration?"

Emma threw her arms in the air. "Ice cream, ice cream, you're our man! We will eat you if we can!"

Jonathan looked at Laura with a *yikes* kind of smile on his face and mouthed, "Where does she get this stuff?"

Laura gave an exaggerated shrug, mouthing back, "I have no idea."

"Ice cream, ice cream, you're our guy! If I don't eat you, I will cry!"

Jonathan scooped Emma into his arms. "We can't have that, Tiny! No tears when you win the big game!"

"So we get ice cream?"

He looked to Laura for permission. She gave him a thumbs-up. "We get ice cream," he confirmed.

"Yay!"

They walked over to The Sundae School, housed in a cedar-shingled store that was designed to look like an old-fashioned ice cream parlor, with an old-school soda fountain and colorful ice-cream signs from the '50s and '60s—five-cent cones and thirty-cent sundaes—lining the walls.

Jonathan ordered a hot-fudge sundae for Emma, a scoop of mocha crunch for Laura and, for himself, he chose a waffle cone with a double scoop of a gourmet rocky road, complete with roasted almonds, chocolate chunks and swirls of fudge. When he took his first taste, he groaned. "I'm going to pack on twenty pounds if I stay here much longer."

"Just named one of the best ice cream spots on the whole Cape," Laura said.

He groaned again. "I believe it."

Emma already had whipped cream on her nose. "I love ice cream," she said happily. Jonathan reached over with a napkin and wiped her face.

"You girls want to go mini golfing after this?"

"Yeah!" Emma cheered.

Laura cocked her head to the side. "I thought you had to work."

He shrugged. "It's Sunday. It can wait."

They walked back to church and picked up Laura's car, then drove the few minutes to the mini golf course, Davy Jones's Locker. "I haven't been mini golfing since high school," Jonathan said, looking around.

The course was well-done, full of fake pirate ships, plastic sharks and rusty anchors. In a small pond under a waterfall, they could even see the scaly green back of the Loch Ness Monster.

"Laura Lessoway. As I live and breathe!" the middle-aged woman behind the counter greeted them. She was wearing a T-shirt with a picture of a golf ball set atop a golf tee and the saying Tee Shirt written across her chest.

"Hi, Darlene," Laura said.

"And little Emma! Hello, sweetheart."

"Hi, Mrs. Darween."

"How are you doing without your dear grandmother?" the woman asked.

"You know," Laura replied. "Hanging in."

"Well, we just opened last weekend. This game's on the house."

"Oh, you don't have to do that," Laura protested. Darlene was a member of the congregation at WCC.

When Gram had passed, she'd dropped off a casserole at the inn.

"Don't worry about it, honey. You and your young man enjoy your game," Darlene said, winking at Jonathan.

"Oh, he's not—"

The older woman cut her off by handing them their putters and balls. She was almost as bad as Chloe. "See you in church next weekend."

"See you there."

They walked to the first tee and watched Emma whack her ball like it was a hockey puck. "Not so hard, honey," Laura called after her.

"You weren't kidding about this being a tight-knit community," Jonathan said. It looked like he was fighting back a smile.

Laura sighed. He'd caught Darlene's not-so-subtle attempt at matchmaking. "Sorry about that."

After Emma sank her ball, he lined up his putt. "She's looking out for you," he teased. "I think it's sweet." His ball hugged the rim of the hole, then lipped out.

"Mr. Jonafin! You almost got a hole in one!"

"There's no *almost* in golf, Tiny. It's either in or it's out." But Emma wasn't listening; she'd already moved on to the next hole.

Laura shot and bounced her ball off an obstacle on the course. "What did you think of the service this morning?"

He twirled his putter. "A little different from the church I grew up in."

"Oh, yeah?"

"Ours was more traditional," he said. "You know, organ player, old-school hymns."

"Right."

He lined up his next shot. "I see why you like it, though. There's a lot of energy. And the people seem nice."

Now it was her turn to tease. "So, if you don't go to church and you don't play mini golf, what *do* you do in your spare time?"

He laughed. "What spare time?"

"Oh, come on," she said. "Nothing?"

"I go to a lot of networking events. I run the occasional 10K. Other than that, I work."

"I used to run, too," she said, "before Emma. But no organized races."

"Why not?"

She hit her ball. "That makes it about the competition, not the joy."

He looked at her, and there was something in his eyes—something almost *reverent*—that made her swallow hard.

She liked him. She did. He was easy to talk to, he was smart, he was good-looking. And, boy, if the way he was with Emma was any indication, he'd make a fantastic father someday.

But he was also ambitious and career driven, and he would run her over in his pursuit to make partner if he had to. He'd spent twenty years on the path to partnership, he'd told her last night, sacrificed nights and vacations and holidays. Maybe he hadn't sacrificed a marriage, like Conrad had, but who knew what he would do in time?

He retrieved his ball from the hole and they walked to the next one. "Nate invited me over to watch a hockey game on Wednesday night."

"Another fanboy for their sports club, huh?"

"You don't like hockey?" he asked.

She shrugged. "Never really watched it."

"We should go to a game sometime. It's fun."

"Hockey. Meh," she said. "But if you want to go see the Red Sox…" What was she *doing*? After her conversation with Chloe at church, she was supremely aware that she was flirting, and based on the way Jonathan's eyes were glued to her, she was pretty sure she was doing a more than adequate job.

Why, though? She wasn't the kind of woman who played games with men. And if Jonathan was even half as committed to his job as her father was to his, she wasn't interested, even if he did treat Emma like the daughter he'd never had.

Or was she?

She bit her lip again. He didn't take himself too seriously, unlike the other corporate men she'd known. He was real, too, and very considerate. She hadn't missed the fact that, after Darlene comped their game, Jonathan had stuffed a twenty-dollar bill into the tip jar on the counter.

He pulled out his phone. "On it. I'm checking for tickets right now."

She laughed. "Oh, no, don't do that. I can't take the time away from the inn. Not with the summer season starting up." She didn't want to lead him on, not when she knew for a fact that they'd never be the right fit.

"Of course." He put his phone away and lined up his next putt. He missed by a mile. "Some other time."

She nodded. "Some other time." She made her shot and sank it—a hole in one.

"Nice!" He held out his hand for a high five. She slapped it. Then he pointed his putter down the street like a divining rod. "Next stop, fried clams."

On the ride home after dinner at the clam shack, Laura told Jonathan she was going out.

"Hot date?" He tried to keep his voice casual, but it was hard. After she'd turned him down on the Red Sox game, it was definitely hard.

Given the fact that she had Tiny to watch out for, he understood why she'd said no, although it left him feeling curiously disappointed. There was something about her that made him want to be the man she could trust with anything, with everything—her daughter, her feelings, her heart.

Was it fair, though, if he was leaving? Was it fair when he was so dedicated to his job? Surely they could try to do things long-distance, couldn't they? And after the sale of The Sea Glass Inn went through, maybe he could convince her to move to Boston to be closer to him.

All he knew was that he couldn't let the details cloud the fact that he hadn't felt this way about anyone *ever*, and that if she was going out with some other man tonight, it would feel like a stake shoved straight through his heart.

She shook her head, a smile quirking her lips. "Brett's got his youth ministry. I've got mine."

"Okay, now I'm curious," he said as they pulled up in front of the inn.

"I was just going to drop you off before heading out, but if you want to come, we can always use more male volunteers…"

"Uh-oh. What am I getting myself into?"

"You know how those little kids at ball hockey loved you?" she asked. He nodded. "Be prepared for the absolute opposite with our surly teens."

They got to WCC and dropped Emma off at the babysitting room in the main church before walking over to the church annex. Outside, the crickets were out in force, as were the peeper frogs, their calls like mini alarms. Unlike in Boston, there was no background whir of cars and trucks and subway trains to drown out the indigenous sounds. Just the peeps and the chirps and their footfalls on the ground.

"Have you heard of Celebrate Recovery before?" Laura asked.

"You mentioned it the other night, didn't you?" he said, opening the door to the church annex for her.

"It's pretty cool. It's a recovery program for everyone, for whatever issue they're struggling with—alcohol, drugs, codependency, divorce, you name it."

"Ah," he said. "Is that how you got involved? After your divorce?"

"Actually, no. It was when I was a teenager, here for the summer after my parents took off. It's why I've got such a heart for the teen ministry. Because I get it, what it feels like to struggle at that age."

"Your parents?" he asked gently.

She bit her lip, nodded. "I guess they thought I was

too old to come to Hong Kong, or I'd do better here, or something. I don't know. But I felt bad about it for a long time. Like, what's wrong with me that they'd leave me behind?"

"What's wrong with *you*?" he scoffed.

"Yeah," she said. "That's why I value the church community so much. They're the ones who helped me see that if I'm right with God, nothing else matters. No one can make me feel inferior or invisible. No one can make me feel like I'm not enough. My identity isn't wrapped up in where I'm from or who raised me or what I've achieved. I'm a child of God, and that's a pretty awesome thing to be."

Jonathan looked at her intently. "You're amazing," he said, and he meant it. She was incredible, this beautiful woman. No wonder she'd said, that first night they'd met, that the word *nice* didn't even begin to describe her faith. *Transformative* was more like it. He wondered what it would be like to be so secure in the knowledge of God's grace.

She shook her head. "It's not me. You'll see. Come to these meetings long enough and you start to see that God can work a miracle in anyone's life."

They were at the door to the meeting room, a handful of kids clustered on an old brown couch, a handful playing foosball at a beat-up table in the back.

"Hey, everyone," Laura said. The kids looked up, waved or said hello. "This is my friend Jonathan. He's going to help out tonight." There were a few "heys" and head nods directed at him. "Let's get started. Who wants to pray?"

Pretty soon, Laura was walking the kids through

a lesson on powerlessness—how God doesn't have space to work his healing power until a person stops denying his pain, and stops trying to control his own life and emotions.

"So, you guys know Matthew 6:24, right? Where Jesus says no one can serve two masters?

"Jesus was talking about money here, but the verse really applies to *anything* you place before God in your life—even your pain, your addictions or your bad habits, right? Like, for me, it was resentment toward my parents. For a while, putting the blame on them made me feel better about myself. But pretty soon that resentment got out of control. It was all I could see, and then I was depressed and unhappy all the time. The thing I thought I had control over started to control me."

The kids nodded, and then split up into a group of boys and a group of girls for the "open share" portion of the evening. Jonathan joined another male volunteer in listening to the boys. One of them was upset that his girlfriend had broken up with him. Another talked about how much he hated his acne. And then there was the boy whose mother was a drug addict, who lived with his aunt and whose older brother had just gotten arrested for using a fake ID to try to buy alcohol.

"My aunt is threatening to kick him out," the kid said miserably. "She says he made his bed and now he needs to lie in it. Learn to live with the consequences of his actions, unlike our mother, who, according to Aunt Rose, avoids responsibility for everything in her life."

One of the rules for open share was that there was

no cross talk, and Jonathan had to bite his tongue until the group let out.

"Hey," Jonathan said, hurrying to catch the kid before he headed out with his friends. "Dan, was it?"

The kid looked at him warily. He was maybe fifteen, tall and thin in that way of teen boys who sprout six inches in less than a year. "Hey."

"Your brother. Has he gotten in trouble before? With the law?"

The kid shook his head. "No, man. Never even had a detention at school. He's supposed to go to UMass in the fall."

Jonathan took a business card out of his wallet, scribbled his cell number on the back. "I'm a lawyer. You want help with this, you let me know."

The kid took the card, his skepticism written all over his face. "We don't have a lot of money for lawyers."

"You wouldn't be retaining me to be his defense attorney. But I know some people. If you want, I could make a few calls."

"Um, yeah, sure, okay. But why me? Why us?"

Jonathan wasn't really sure he wanted to have this conversation, but the kid had opened up about his life during the sharing portion of the meeting; he figured there was no way this boy would trust him if he didn't do the same. And for some reason—maybe because his search for his father had brought old memories and feelings to the fore, and maybe because he was still determined to show Laura that not all lawyers were the unethical, morally bankrupt people she thought they were—he really wanted this kid to trust him.

"I get it," Jonathan said, "what it's like to have a parent who's got a mental illness."

"Oh, yeah?" the kid asked.

"Yeah, it was my dad. Bipolar disorder. He never wanted to take his meds. Disappeared on us when I was about your brother's age, about to head off to college. It messes you up."

The kid stared at his feet. "My mom hasn't really been in the picture since I was in grade school."

"That's a raw deal," Jonathan said.

The kid toed the floor with his scuffed-up shoe. "Ethan took care of me when Mom left. We were alone for like a week before DCF got involved and took us to Aunt Rose." The boy looked away, his voice dropping to a whisper. "We've been reading about it all weekend, man. He could go to jail for three months. He could lose his financial aid package. My aunt said once he graduates from high school, he's on his own. I'm scared about what's gonna happen to him."

Jonathan touched the kid on the elbow. "Here, let's sit down so you can tell me everything I need to know about Ethan. I'm going to do my best to make sure nothing bad goes down."

Chapter Eleven

"I don't get it, Harvard. I thought you were a corporate lawyer, not a criminal one." Laura studied him over her cup of coffee in the dining room on Monday morning. He was dressed for court: suit, tie, cuff links, the whole deal. She'd already dropped Emma off at preschool; he'd been on the phone when she'd left, and on the phone when she'd returned. In fact, he'd been on the phone half the night—with former classmates, he'd told her, and people within his extended professional network—trying to figure out a way to help this Ethan kid.

This morning, he'd told her, he'd already spoken with the juvenile police prosecutor, the assistant district attorney assigned to Ethan's case and the head of the Juvenile Diversion Program—which, as he'd explained it to her, was an alternate to arrest that included counseling and community service.

"I know," he said, "I'm not, but my friend Constantine—"

"The criminal defense lawyer?" she asked.

He nodded. "Yeah, he can't get down here today

for the arraignment, and I need to be there to ask for a continuance so we can try to get Ethan into the Juvenile Diversion Program."

"You know one of the Celebrate Recovery guidelines is that we're there to support one another, not fix one another," she said. "This seems like a pretty big fix."

"You really want a seventeen-year-old, straight-A student to have a permanent mark on his record from trying to use a fake ID?" he asked.

"No, but—"

"Their mom took off on them when they were in grade school, Laura. Their aunt barely tolerates their presence. These kids could use a break."

"I get it, I do, I just worry that maybe you're getting a little overinvolved…"

She saw a muscle in his jaw tighten. "I'm trying to do something nice here."

"I know you are, I know," she soothed. "And if it works out, those boys will definitely appreciate it. I guess I'm just worried about—well, what if it doesn't work out? What if you promised more than you can deliver?"

He smirked. "You don't make it to the top corporate law firm in Boston without being able to deliver on your promises."

She lifted an eyebrow. "Why are you so invested in this whole thing?"

"Lawyers are competitive," he said easily. "I like to win."

She shook her finger at him. "Uh-uh, Harvard. You're not getting off the hook that easy. What's the real reason?"

"The real reason?" He glanced up at ceiling. "Man, you're relentless."

She waited, head cocked.

He blew out a breath. "I used to wish my dad had cancer instead of bipolar disorder, because at least with cancer, there's a way to cure it. You can do surgery, you can do chemo, you can do radiation. But you can't go in and cut the mental illness out of someone's head."

Laura reached out, laid her hand on his arm. Her heart hurt for him. "I can't imagine."

"I coped with it by throwing myself into school. But I get it—why some kids might act out." He hesitated for a moment. "I don't want this kid to pay for this for the rest of his life. You get a criminal record, even for a misdemeanor, they can rescind your acceptance at college. They can cancel your financial aid. I don't think one mistake should warrant those kinds of consequences."

He looked at where her hand rested on his arm, then into her eyes. "It's kind of like what you were talking about last night, about your church community being there for you. Maybe I want to be part of extending this kid a little bit of grace."

They were silent for a moment—not a charged silence, but a contemplative one. "Your dad," Laura said finally. "Did he try to get help? I mean, I know he was hospitalized, but was it voluntary, or did you guys have to commit him?"

Jonathan gave a humorless laugh. "Bit of both, I guess. Sometimes it was his idea, but he never stuck with his treatment. Said the drugs made him feel dead inside. He loved the mania, loved the high. He thought he could control it himself, like there was some magical off button that would stop it from tipping over into chaos." He shook his head. "And then the depression that would follow was brutal. Just brutal. There were times he'd go out and wouldn't come home for days. I was always afraid something terrible would happen…"

The bleakness in his voice nearly killed her.

"And then he just disappeared into thin air. All these years, we've had to wonder, had to worry…" He put his hand over his eyes and shook his head a little, obviously trying to get his emotions in check.

She gave him a moment to collect himself, then took his other hand and squeezed it. "You're doing a good thing for that kid, Harvard."

He took a deep breath, removed his hand from his face and looked at her. "Yeah?"

She nodded. "Yeah." He had that same shaky, vulnerable look in his eyes that he'd had the night they'd gone to Beacon Light, and she couldn't help it, she had to offer him comfort. "I hope you don't think this is weird, but can I give you a hug?"

She saw his face crack into a lopsided smile and she felt…happy. Useful. Like she had a role to play in easing his burdens, at least for a little while.

"I definitely think it's weird, Lessoway," he said, seeming to instinctively know that she needed there to be a bit of levity in this exchange, "but come here."

He opened his arms and tucked her into a big bear hug.

As Jonathan drove back to the inn from the arraignment hearing, he felt happier about his day's work than he'd felt in a long time. He'd been able to get the continuance they needed so that the Juvenile Diversion Program could evaluate Ethan and make a determination on whether to accept him into the program.

Helping an actual person instead of a corporation was strangely gratifying. He'd never been particularly interested in criminal law—being a defense attorney meant working for liars and criminals, and being a prosecutor meant seeing humanity at its absolute worst from day in to day out—but maybe there were some other options out there. Immigration law or adoption law, something where you helped good people who hadn't broken the law but who simply needed help.

But he couldn't seriously be considering giving up his prestigious job with the best corporate law firm in Boston to look into becoming a solo practitioner in an area of law he hadn't touched since law school, could he?

Rain started falling, and he picked up his speed. If Laura needed to get the roof repaired, she wouldn't be happy about this storm. He wondered if the ceiling in his room was going to leak onto his bed.

He ran from his car to the inn with his briefcase over his head to hold off the rain. Chloe and Emma were in the parlor, playing Go Fish.

"Hey," he said, putting the briefcase down and dusting drops of rain off his jacket. "Where's Laura?"

Chloe looked at him, her mouth drawn into an unhappy line. "On the roof. With some tarp. To try to stop the rain from getting in."

"What?"

"Yeah. I don't know. I couldn't stop her."

He ran back outside, called her name. She didn't answer. His pulse went into warp speed. What if she'd slipped off the roof? What if she'd fallen?

He ran around the side of the inn, saw the ladder and immediately climbed up. His dress shoes had no tread on the bottoms, so he stopped partway up and shed both the shoes and his socks, deciding that bare feet were better than slippery shoes.

When he got to the top, he saw her straightaway. She was draped over the ridge of the roof, one arm and leg on one side of the slope, one arm and leg on the other. She was facing away from him and the sound of the rain was loud, so he doubted she knew he was there.

"Laura," he called out, "it's Jonathan. Don't move. I'm going to get you down."

"Jonathan, it's too slippery!" she cried, and he could hear the terror in her voice. "I'm going to fall!"

His eyes scanned the roof. Her right foot really wasn't that far from him. He was pretty sure that if he just shimmied up a little, he could grab her.

But if he was wrong, and they both slipped, then what? He wouldn't be able to live with himself if she got hurt on his watch.

"You're not going to fall, sweetheart. Just stay right where you are. I'm going to go tell Chloe to call 911, okay? I'll be right back."

He hurried down the ladder and around to the front of the inn, threw the front door open and barked at Chloe to call 911. He saw Emma's eyes go wide and frightened, and he gentled his voice. "It's okay, honey, everything's okay. Your mommy's not hurt, just stuck, and the firemen are going to come and help her."

The little girl nodded, and he ran back into the rain and up the ladder. Laura was right where she'd been when he'd left her, and he felt a surge of relief so strong it would have knocked him over if he didn't already have so much adrenaline rushing through his veins. "I'm back," he called out. "The fire department's coming."

"Jonathan," she cried. "It's so slippery."

"It's okay, sweetheart. It's okay. I'm here. I'm not going to let you fall." He looked out toward the road, didn't see any lights or hear any sirens. "Can you push yourself back, just a little? It's okay if you can't, but if you can, I might be able to reach you."

He saw her hands move up toward her head, toward the center of the ridge. "I'm scared," she said.

"It's okay. I'm right here. You don't have to move if you don't want to. I'm not going to let anything happen to you."

She pushed herself back a few inches. He reached up and grazed her right heel with his fingertips.

"That's good, sweetheart. That's good. Push yourself back a little bit more and I'll be able to get you."

She moved back again and his hand encircled her ankle. "See? There. Now I've got you. Can you push yourself back a little more?" She did it, and he moved his hand to her calf. "Okay, now bring your left leg over the top slowly—really slow, honey. I've got you. Just like that."

She managed to creep her other leg over, and he used his hands to pull her closer to him, then inch her down the slope. He could hear her whimpering now, see that she had her eyes closed tight. "You're okay," he said. "I've got you."

He took a slow step down the ladder, still holding on to her, though he had her by the hips now, not the feet. "Laura, I'm going to guide your feet to the ladder, okay? Do you think you can climb down?"

"I...I don't know," she stuttered. Her teeth were chattering. Her face was very white.

"You can do it, sweetheart. I've got you. We'll do it together, okay? Just one step at a time."

He guided her feet to the ladder, then reached up to steady her waist. "Come on, honey. One step. Use your right foot," he told her. "Good," he breathed when she carefully, carefully started to make her way down. "Now your left."

They crept down the ladder, his heart in his throat the whole time. When they got to the bottom, she collapsed into him, sobbing.

"I've got you, I've got you," he murmured, clutching her to his chest. "You're okay. It's over. I've got you."

A fire truck pulled up to the curb in a blaze of sound and light, followed by an ambulance. Jonathan led Laura over to the paramedics. "We got her down," he informed the first responders. "I think she's just in a little bit of shock."

The paramedics sat her down inside the ambulance bay, wrapped a blanket around her shoulders and started a quick exam.

"Want us to look at your feet, man?" one of the guys asked him.

Jonathan looked down. His feet were bleeding.

"I'm okay. Just take care of her, please. I'm going to go tell her daughter that everything's all right."

Laura sat in the parlor in her fuzzy pink slippers and pink flannel pajamas, nursing a cup of tea. She felt insanely embarrassed. All that fuss with the fire truck and the ambulance and Emma's frightened little face.

And Jonathan.

She groaned—Jonathan. Who'd been so steady, so rock-solid when she was panicking on the roof. *I've got you*, he'd said. *I've got you, I've got you.* And what a relief it had been to hear it each time he'd said it. To know that he was there, that she could count on him. *I won't let you fall.*

What must he think of her and her stupid plan to climb up there in the rain?

As though she'd conjured him with her thoughts, he appeared on the stairs, wearing dry clothes. "Hey," he said gently, descending the steps and sitting beside her on the couch. "How're you feeling?"

She bit her lip. "Stupid," she said. "Embarrassed." Chloe had taken Emma to The Candy Shack to give Laura time to recover, so they were alone.

He took her hand, stroked it with his thumb. "I'm just glad you're okay."

She didn't want to cry again, she really didn't want to, but it was too late. The tears were already spilling down her cheeks.

"Hey." He held her hand more tightly. "It's okay."

"I'm sorry." She held herself rigid, trying to stanch the flow of tears, angrily wiping them from her cheeks with her free hand. "I don't know what's wrong with me."

"You can cry," he said softly. "It was scary up there in the rain. It's okay to cry."

"I hardly even know you!" she protested, although—strangely enough—the words didn't ring true. After everything they'd been through over the last few days, she felt like she *did* know him, had perhaps *always* known him, even though, objectively, it had been less than a week.

He let go of her hand, wrapped his arm around her shoulder and pulled her close to his side. "You know me," he said.

And then she was sobbing, her body curled into his, her breaths a violent staccato against his chest, her face soaking his shirt with saliva and tears.

After what seemed like an eternity, she took in a deep, shuddering breath and inched backward. "I'm sorry," she whispered. It was hard to draw away from him—she felt the pull of him, of his fresh, clean scent, his protective warmth, his comforting touch.

He kept his arm around her shoulders. "Don't be sorry," he said. "I'm here. It's okay."

She wiped at her face. "It's just—I miss Gram so much. And everything's changing, everything's falling apart, and I thought—I thought..."

"You thought maybe you could fix it," he said simply. "I get it. It's okay."

She craned her head to look at him. He gave her a crooked smile. "I have big shoulders. I promise you I can take a few sniffles."

She wiped at her face again, which was tingling.

It was strange, given that she'd just had a meltdown in front of him, but his teasing actually made her feel better. "A few, huh?"

He nodded solemnly, dark eyes dancing. "I do have a younger sister, you know."

"So you've seen your share of sniffles?"

He gave her another lopsided smile. "I've seen my share of sniffles."

She took a breath. She liked the weight of his arm on her shoulders. She liked the way he'd held her when she'd cried. She liked knowing that she could fall apart without fear that he'd judge her. She liked knowing that strong emotions wouldn't scare him away…even if he *was* a workaholic lawyer who liked wearing fancy suits to the beach.

She ducked her face into his shoulder and whispered, "Thank you, Harvard."

"Anytime, Lessoway." He gave her shoulder a squeeze. "You need me, I'm there."

Chapter Twelve

Laura was psyched. After she'd dropped Emma off at preschool, she'd gone to talk to a restaurant owner friend of Chloe's about her web design services, and she'd gotten the job!

She couldn't wait to tell Jonathan. He was such a good guy. The *best*. After she'd sobbed all over him last night, he'd helped her clean up the water that had leaked in through the roof, and this morning, before she and Emma were even up, he'd gotten more tarp and gone up and fastened it over the problem spots on the roof.

He'd called her sweetheart yesterday. He'd let her cry on his chest. Did that mean…? Maybe it meant…

Her excitement came to an abrupt halt, however, when she walked in the front door of the inn and found Jonathan sitting in the parlor with her mother, laughing as though Eleanor were the world's great wit.

"Darling!" her mother cried, large, sparkling diamonds shining from her ears, wrists and throat. "I'm back!"

"Hey, Mom," Laura replied warily, taking in her mother's trim figure, her perfectly styled hair, her designer clothes.

While her father had spent most of his time at the office when she and her sisters were growing up, their mother had spent many a long hour at the gym, doing Pilates and yoga. And when she wasn't at the gym, she was shopping or getting a manicure or discussing the pros and cons of Botox with her friends from the country club.

Not for the first time, Laura thanked God for her grandmother's influence in her life. *For where your treasure is, there will your heart be also.* Thanks to Gram, Laura knew exactly where her treasure was, and it wasn't in a fat bank account or a thin body or a pretty face.

It was here, at the inn, with the memory of people she loved, and people who had loved her.

"How was your trip?" she asked her mom.

"Wonderful, darling. So rejuvenating. They really do the spa right at the Ritz-Carlton, and Newbury Street is so pretty this time of year. The cherry blossoms have just exploded. You should go up there, darling. Spend some of your inheritance. Take a break."

"Mom," she said slowly, aware that Jonathan was in the room, aware that she had information he didn't. "You know there won't be an inheritance unless we meet the terms of the will."

Out of the corner of her eye, she saw Jonathan's head snap up at that. Felt his gaze fix on her face.

Her stomach dropped. She should have told him.

She should have gotten him those documents when he'd first asked, instead of dragging it out for days.

"This one," her mother said, speaking to Jonathan but waving her hand in Laura's direction, "always the worrier. Always so good at managing the details, but the big picture?" She turned and looked abruptly at Laura. "So not your strong suit, darling."

"Mom," Laura said, a warning, but her voice was too quiet.

Her mother kept right on talking: "Her father was always so proud of her. And then she had to go and drop out of college."

"Mom," she said again. "Please stop."

"You'd think she'd be happy about selling this old place and starting over somewhere fresh, but no, not our Laura. She has to throw a wrench in the works every time."

"Mom! Please!"

"Oh, Jonathan doesn't mind, do you, Handsome?" Her mother patted him on the cheek. He looked dumbfounded.

"Actually," he said, looking straight at Laura, the look in his eyes detached, somehow, even cold, "I'd like to see a copy of the will."

Her heart was hammering in her chest. This wasn't the same guy who'd helped her off the roof yesterday. This wasn't vacation-mode Jonathan, this was work-mode Jonathan, and work-mode Jonathan was as impersonal as ice. "I have to go. I have to get Emma from preschool."

"Run along, darling." Her mother smiled. Her teeth looked sharp as knives.

* * *

Jonathan sat at a table in the inn's front yard, watching the American flag on the flagpole flap in the wind. He wasn't wearing a suit today, just black jeans and a red polo shirt. He had to admit, despite having met Eleanor in Boston and despite everything Laura had told him about her childhood, he hadn't been expecting all the drama, and he felt more than a little confused.

Laura had been putting him off about finding the documents he needed for his due diligence for almost a week now, implying that it would be easier to find them if they waited until her mother was in town. Not that he'd been pushing too hard lately, but that was neither here nor there...

But Eleanor had no idea where to find the information he needed. According to her, she'd barely set foot in The Sea Glass Inn since she'd moved to Hong Kong. She hated the inn—she'd always hated the inn, she'd told him. She hadn't even lived here when her parents had first bought it, when she was still a teen.

Jonathan didn't really know what to do with that information. He knew Laura loved this place. He liked it, too. But why was she dragging her feet on compiling the documents he needed? Didn't she understand how much money Carberry Hotels wanted to throw at her? She and Emma would be able to go anywhere, do anything. If she invested the money wisely, as he had no doubt she would, she'd never have to work again a day in her life.

So what was the hold-up? Why the delay?

Was she just trying to irritate her mother? Or did those documents contain material information she didn't want him to know? Debts, liens, pending litigation? Man, if he'd wasted nearly a week here for nothing…

He rubbed his temples. He felt a headache coming on.

Not that he hadn't enjoyed goofing off with her and Emma for the past few days. He had. No doubt. Even with the disappointment of not finding his father and the terrible anxiety of yesterday afternoon, it had been the most relaxing few days he could remember in a long time.

But he didn't need to relax right now. He needed to focus. Because once he'd drafted the legal agreements associated with this deal, he could set his sights on wooing Carberry Hotels over to his law firm. And if he was successful, he'd soon hold his partnership in the palm of his hand.

He took out his phone to bring Mike Roe up to speed on the situation at the inn.

"Masters," Mike said in greeting. "What's the word? We got ourselves a deal?"

Jonathan shook his head. "Hit a snag."

"What's up? Thought you'd have this one in the bag by now." At a holiday party a couple of years ago, someone had described Mike as "festive." Jonathan had always thought that description was particularly apt. When everything went Mike's way he was the life of the party, and his perfectionism ensured that things went his way most of the time. But if perchance you messed up on one of his cases, you basically ceased to exist for him, and you never got a second shot at earning your way back into his good graces.

Mentally, Jonathan tried to prepare himself for the moment Mike's sun ceased to shine. He'd been Mike's go-to guy for years now, and without Mike's special favor, would he even recognize himself? "I'm having a little trouble getting the documents together for the initial review."

"And it took you, what? Six days to realize this? A week?"

Jonathan opened his mouth, then closed it again. He'd gotten distracted. He knew it. No need for Mike to rub it in.

"It's not going to probate court, is it? That would put this thing on ice for months and months."

"I don't think so…"

"You don't *think* so, Masters? Haven't you seen the will?"

Jonathan shook his head, though Mike couldn't see him. He hadn't seen the will.

Mike let out a bark of sarcastic laughter. "What have you been doing down there? You meet a girl?"

Jonathan's silence was all the confirmation Mike needed. "You did. You met a girl. Great. Fantastic. Just what I need. I thought I could count on you, Masters. Do I have to find somebody else to take care of this for me?"

Jonathan gritted his teeth. If Mike had to send someone else down here, it would be career suicide. "I'll get it done."

"See that you do," Mike ordered. Then he hung up.

Jonathan put the phone down, rubbed his face. This was a mess. He needed to see those documents.

He needed to see if Laura was hiding something. He needed to see the will. Now.

A car pulled up in front of the inn. Emma hopped out, followed closely by Chloe and then, more slowly, Laura.

"Mr. Jonafin!" Emma yelled, running over.

"Hey, Tiny." He worked hard to make his voice sound normal.

"Aunt Chloe's gonna take me to the beach to look for seashells!" she exclaimed, while Chloe gave him a sheepish wave. It appeared that Laura had filled her in on all the fun with her mom. "Do you wanna come?" Emma asked.

"Not right now, Tiny. But thanks." Talking to her as though everything was normal left him feeling lost. Bereft.

"We're gonna go get my sand buckets and shovels," Emma announced, dragging Chloe away by the hand.

Laura approached him slowly, like an animal wary of a predator. "Hey, um, about earlier—"

"Your mother doesn't know where to find my documents." His voice sounded flat.

Her face froze for a second.

"I'm betting you know exactly where they are, don't you?" He stood so he wouldn't have to look up at her.

She lifted her chin defiantly. "I told you I'd get to it when I have time."

"Gee, thanks. And when's that going to be? Today? Tomorrow? Next week?" He heard the sarcasm, but couldn't stop it. Mike thought he had to send someone else down here to do Jonathan's job. He'd never been the unreliable one before. He'd always been sharp and disciplined and focused. Why couldn't he be that way now?

"You want them now?" She gestured indignantly toward the front door. "We can get them now."

"Finally. You do realize that I've been here a week now, and I have nothing to show for it."

She regarded him steadily. "Nothing, huh?"

He felt his jaw tighten. "Is there something in those documents you don't want me to see? A debt? A lien? A lawsuit?"

She flinched. "Is that what you think of me?"

"Well, what am I supposed to think, Laura?" His voice was clipped. He didn't understand why this woman—this gorgeous, smart, *captivating* woman— was standing between him and his goals. He'd told her how important this was to him. It wasn't as though she didn't know that his career was on the line. "Here I want to give you a boatload of money, and you've been stalling this whole time."

"You think that's what's important to me? Money?" She shook her head, her hands fisted on her hips, her eyes full of...pity. "You're as bad as my mother."

"You know, it would have been nice if you'd given me a heads-up earlier that this whole trip would just be a big waste of my time."

Her green eyes flashed, the pity turning hurt and wild. "Oh, what? Me telling you the inn wasn't for sale and slamming the door in your face wasn't a big enough clue that *I didn't want you here*?"

"You let me back in, Laura! You let me believe..." Instead of finishing his sentence, he stared toward the beach, where the grass waved on the dunes and the waves crashed on the shore and the light from the jetty flashed faithfully—mockingly—reminding him of how stupid he'd been to put his faith in anyone beside himself.

"What?" she demanded. "I let you believe what?"

He shoved his hands in his pockets. She'd let him believe a lot of things, but nothing he wanted to talk about now. "Nothing. Never mind. Let's get the documents. Let's go."

Chapter Thirteen

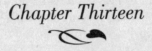

Laura sifted some sand through her fingers, looking for little shells. Chloe and Emma were closer to the water, shoes off, squealing every time a wave broke at their feet.

She surveyed the coastline around her. It was *very* different here from Hong Kong's Repulse Bay. There, restaurants lined the beachfront, crammed with people from morning to night, especially on the weekends. It was a place for young professionals to see and be seen, a place for hired help to take other people's children. Here, though, was a place for families.

Yes, the public beach here got crowded in the summer, but it wasn't a trendy crowd. It wasn't a bunch of nannies hanging out together while their young charges amused themselves in the sand. It was parents building memories with their children, alongside the sand castles. It was knowing, deep down, that while the memories might be built on sand, the family making them most certainly wasn't.

She sighed, feeling both sad and angry, but she

wasn't sure where to direct her anger—at her mother, at Jonathan or at herself?

She'd been taken aback to see him in the parlor with her mother, that was for sure. And the shock, the coolness in his eyes after he'd found out about the will…

He'd told her, that first night, why he was there. He'd told her again and again—every time he asked her to pull together the documents for his review. But still, her foolish heart had glossed right over all the warning signs. Her foolish heart had wanted…more.

Sure, she'd given good lip service to not wanting to be with him. To Angie, to Chloe, to herself, it had been deny, deny, deny. But in her heart of hearts, she'd wanted him to be the man she'd seen over the last few days. The one who confided in her, the one who comforted her, the one who made her daughter shine with joy. The man he was when he relaxed a little. The man he was without the cutthroat, high-stakes job.

Obviously, though, he was not that man. Because, when push came to shove, she was just a *big waste of his time*.

She bit her lip. Hard. She wasn't an angel in all this. She'd purposefully kept him from looking at those documents, and she wasn't even entirely sure why. She'd always known he'd see them eventually, always known that, if her mother had her heart set on selling, there really wasn't anything she could do to block the sale. She certainly didn't have the money to buy out her mother's share of The Sea Glass Inn. So, if Carberry Hotels was where this thing was heading, she supposed Carberry Hotels was where it would have to be.

And telling Jonathan she didn't want him here? A

lie. Maybe it had been true that first night, before she'd gotten to know him. At that point, she truly *hadn't* wanted some smarmy lawyer hanging around trying to lay claim to the inn.

But that had been before she'd talked to him, before she'd told him about Conrad, and her dad, and her fears for Emma's future. Before he'd fixed her dishwasher, and rescued her from falling off the roof. Before she'd started to believe that maybe, just maybe, not all lawyers were the unethical, morally bankrupt people she'd believed them to be.

I've been here a week now, and you've been stalling this whole time.

She'd known, back at the trampoline park, even on the drive to Beacon Light, that she was in trouble, in danger of falling for him. But if that was how he felt about the past few days, that it was all a big *nothing*, then maybe she could let go of those worries. Because, clearly, he wasn't the man she'd believed him to be.

If only her mother hadn't come back so suddenly. If only she'd had time to talk to him first about the inn, and the will, and why she'd been so hesitant to help him with his deal. She massaged her temples. Why was it always so much easier to be calm when her mother was half a world away?

Laura sighed. Why had her grandmother thought they could run the inn together, even for just a few months? Her mother was self-absorbed and unreliable. They'd drive each other crazy before the season even kicked off on Memorial Day.

Emma squealed and ran up to her. "Mom! Mom! I

got a sand crab!" She was holding the poor burrowing creature in her hands. "It tickles! It tickles!"

Laura held out her hand and Emma dumped the little crab in. "He likes the wet sand, okay, honey?"

"But I want to keep him! I'll put him in my bucket!"

"You can put him in your bucket until we leave, but then you have to let him go."

Emma balanced on one foot like a flamingo for all of five seconds, then tried again on the other foot. "Aw, why? He can be my pet!"

"Honey, he gets his food at the beach," Laura said. "If you leave him in your bucket, he'll die."

"I'll feed him! I'll bring him food every day!" her daughter protested.

"His food's too small for you see, sweetie."

Emma pouted.

"Are you cold, honey? Looks like you got wet."

Emma glanced down at her soggy pants. "I'm not cold."

"Aunt Chloe looks cold."

Chloe turned and waved at them, the bottom of her oversize sweater flapping in the wind. "Some crazy person's out there swimming," she called back to them.

Laura got to her feet, sand crab still in hand, and squinted out to sea. Sure enough, after a minute, she saw the swimmer's strong arms coming out of the water at forty-five-degree angles. Whoever it was, he was out pretty far.

"I want to go swimming!" Emma declared.

"No, honey. The water can't be more than forty degrees. It's too cold."

"Aw. How come they get to go?"

"I'll take you swimming in the summer, cutie pie," Chloe said, "once the water's warm as a bathtub." She bopped Emma on the nose.

"You can't drink ocean water," Emma said, scrunching her face. "It's too salty."

"Do you drink your bathwater?" Chloe asked.

Emma cast a sly glance at Laura. "When Mom's not looking, I pretend to be a whale!"

Laura's eyes tracked the swimmer. "They're almost out to the buoys. They could get hit by a boat."

Chloe shrugged. "Not many boats out there today. I'm sure it'll be fine."

The swimmer turned and headed for shore, which was a relief. There were no lifeguards on duty during the off-season, and if the swimmer had gotten in trouble, she didn't know what they'd have done.

He came out of the ocean about fifty yards away from them. He wasn't wearing a wet suit. Upon exiting the water, he stumbled, and sat down hard on the sand.

"Mr. Jonafin!" Emma yelled, taking off toward him across the sand.

"Honey, that's not—" But she stopped when the swimmer looked up at Emma, because it was him.

It was Jonathan.

Jonathan had done polar bear swims before. For the last five years, he'd done one in Boston Harbor on New Year's Day. It had started as a dare from a coworker, but that coworker was long gone, and Jonathan still made the trek every year.

It was rejuvenating—a shock to the system. After that first swim, he'd actually researched it and discovered that exposure to extreme cold, in short bursts, boosts the production of norepinephrine in the brain, improving mood and alleviating pain.

He felt like he needed those benefits right now.

After Laura had retrieved the documents he needed—*all* the documents, and it had taken only twenty minutes of her time—he'd quickly discovered the thing that would get in the way of the deal: the stipulation in Dorothy's will that Laura and her mother run the inn together for a full summer before it would be released from the trust and put in their names.

Jonathan had called Connor, and he'd been disappointed. He wouldn't be able to get his hands on the inn until at least the fall. Jonathan was disappointed, too. The fall would be too late for Jonathan to redeem himself to Mike by reeling Carberry Hotels into the law firm. And although Connor had said he'd still put in a good word with his father, Jonathan didn't believe it. Connor was almost as unreliable as Jonathan's dad.

Worse than all of that, though, had been the look in Laura's eyes when he'd told her she was wasting his time and she'd replied that *she didn't want him here*.

He got it now, why so many people hated lawyers. He felt like an ambulance chaser, swooping in after the death of her grandmother to offer her a deal she didn't even want.

Prove me wrong, Harvard. Show me that all lawyers aren't the unethical, morally bankrupt people I think you are.

What was wrong with him? The most important deal of his life blows up and all he can think about is her?

Mike was right. He'd gotten distracted by a girl. Now that he knew the Lessoways couldn't sign the contract until the fall, he'd get out of here. Just as soon as he met with Pastor Nate to discuss whether WCC would be open to selling the inn should Dorothy's estate ultimately end up in the hands of the church.

He was, after all, a lawyer. If Laura and her mother managed to kill each other before the summer was up, it was his job to plan for contingencies.

The water was very cold, so cold that he'd gasped in sudden shock upon diving in. Then he'd felt numb to it, robotic as his arms sliced through the waves. But he'd misjudged either the distance to the buoys or the warp and weft of the waves, because it was taking him much longer to get back to shore than he'd anticipated, and he was starting to feel weak from the cold.

When he came out of the water, he felt dazed and fumbling. He went down in the sand before he even had a chance to take note of where he'd come out of the sea.

And then Emma was on top of him, her warm little arms hooked around his neck. "Mr. Jonafin, you're freezy."

"What were you thinking?" Laura cried, skidding to a halt beside him, slapping his arm—hard—her knees in the sand. "You can't go out when the water temperature's this low! You could have killed yourself!"

"I'm fine," he said, teeth chattering. He still felt oddly confused, though, as though he were intoxicated, or this was all a dream.

"Your lips are blue. Where's your towel? Where're your clothes?"

"At the inn," he said. Emma had slid off his lap and he wanted her back—she was like an electric blanket, a ball of heat.

Laura huffed in frustration. "Come on." She levered herself under his arm, motioned for Chloe to do the same on the other side. "Up."

He'd rather have stayed hunched up on the sand, but both women had their arms around his waist, so at least there was some warmth in that.

"Come on," Laura said to Chloe. "Let's get him back to the inn."

Ahead of them, Emma was twirling around and singing "Frosty the Snowman." "That song for me, Tiny?" His voice hitched because he was shivering so hard.

"Mr. Jonafin," she said solemnly, "you should only swim in the bathtub."

They reached the inn and managed to climb the stairs to his room. "You'll take Emma?" Laura asked her friend.

Chloe nodded. "Of course."

Laura pushed him into the bathroom so he could get warm in the shower.

"Do you have any sweats?" she called out to him through the door.

He called back, "Just my track pants and that fleece windbreaker."

"I've got something in lost and found that should fit you."

"Okay."

When he came out of the bathroom, he saw that

she'd left gray sweatpants and a plaid flannel shirt for him on top of his bureau.

He came downstairs a few minutes later.

Emma walked up to him when he got to the bottom of the staircase. "Me and Aunt Chloe maded you some soup." She held a mug out to him.

He took it and sipped. Chicken noodle. Hot. So good. He took a big swallow, felt it warm him from the inside out. "Thanks, Tiny."

"Do you like to be a whale?"

"Hmm?" he said.

"In the tub. You can spout."

"Come on, Em," Chloe said. "We're going to go to Half Shell to help Mr. Brett."

"Okay!" She bounced out the door after Chloe. Laura was sitting in a chair next to the window in the parlor, watching him warily. Nodding toward the flannel shirt, the yellow-and-black-plaid flannel shirt that he'd never in a million years wear under normal circumstances, she said, "Fancy."

He sat on a chair nearby. He still felt cold. "I try."

"I looked up the water temperature today, Harvard. Forty-eight degrees."

He closed his eyes. He didn't like being the unreliable one, the loose cannon. "That was reckless of me. I'm sorry I scared you."

"What were you thinking?" she asked.

He looked out the window behind her. "I wanted to go in the water before I left. I don't know the next time I'll be back on Cape Cod."

"You're leaving?" There was something—and he

could have been reading it wrong, he wasn't sure—a little bit sad, a little bit wistful, in her eyes.

"Can't very well stay here until September to get the contract signed."

"I guess not," she conceded. "When are you leaving?"

"Tomorrow, probably. Or I might wait until Thursday after the hockey game with Brett and Nate."

"That's cool," she said.

"I can head out earlier if you want me to."

She shook her head. "No, no. There's no rush."

He wanted to believe her, but the words *I don't want you here, I don't want you here* were echoing in his head.

"Do you want more soup?" She pushed herself up from her chair. "Let's go to the kitchen."

He got up and followed her. There was a pot of soup on the stove, an empty can beside it. "You mind canned?" she asked.

He shook his head. "I'm not picky."

She turned the heat on—it was gas, not electric— and reheated what was left in the pot. The kitchen had a back door, and there was a cold draft coming in through the cracks. He shivered. "You don't have to take care of me, you know."

She looked at him for a long moment. She was wearing the Red Sox sweatshirt she'd been wearing the night they met. "I know."

He suddenly had a memory of the Christmas he'd been twelve years old, when his father had been in the throes of a manic episode. His father had given him a Rubik's Cube, then gleefully told Jonathan he could solve it in under ten seconds. He'd grabbed a hammer and smashed the Cube to bits.

He remembered how his father thought the house had been bugged and how he'd made Jonathan and his sister, Charlotte, help him go through it with a metal detector. He remembered his dad taking Charlotte by the shoulders and shaking her "to make sure she was really there."

He remembered, hours later, his father pacing, making a triangle sign with his hands and chanting, over and over, "I am a dolphin. I can breathe, but I can't breathe the water." There was no Christmas dinner that year, just a box of macaroni and cheese that he and his sister had made for themselves while their mother was trying to talk their father back into the hospital after another unsuccessful attempt to come off his medication.

He remembered how he had, at twelve years old, made a decision to steel himself against other people, focusing his attention on excelling at school, relying purely on himself to create the future he wanted and leaving nothing to the whims of unpredictable people.

Looking at Laura now, as she puttered at the stove, Jonathan wondered if he was as delusional as his father had been, using his job as a shield against other people, thinking achievement would be the thing to protect him, to prevent him from getting hurt.

Because he was hurting now, and not *in spite* of his job but perhaps *because* of it. And before he'd been hurt by the woman standing in front of him, fetching him soup—well, he was pretty sure he'd hurt her first.

He watched her pour his soup into a mug. "I'm sorry if I scared you," he said again.

She looked up at him, green eyes indecipherable. "You did," she said softly. "Scare me."

She was beautiful, so incredibly sweet and funny and beautiful. He couldn't leave Cape Cod without knowing if she felt for him the way he felt for her.

He stepped closer. She was holding his mug of soup. He took it from her, set it on the aging Formica countertop behind her. Her breathing hitched at his nearness, and he felt hope balloon in his chest. "The way I spoke to you earlier—I'm sorry. I was upset. I took it out on you and I shouldn't have. I said some things I didn't mean."

Her eyes widened and she looked away, made a helpless gesture with her hand. "We both said some things…"

Cupping her face with his hands, forcing her eyes to his, he told her, "Laura. Being here. It hasn't been a waste of time."

She took a shuddering breath, questions pooling in her eyes.

Slowly he took his hands off her face, wanting to kiss her but not wanting to trap her, wanting her to kiss him of her own free will. Slowly he leaned toward her. "I can't stop thinking about you," he said, his voice low.

There was nervousness burning in her eyes, there was fear, but there was an answer shining there, too: *yes*.

Gently, light as a whisper, Jonathan brushed his lips

against hers. A burst of happiness shot through him so fast he felt like he could fly.

He'd never felt like this before. He'd felt attraction, sure, but this overwhelming desire to protect her, keep her smiling and safe? Never. He didn't know what to make of it. He felt like his chest could burst with it. It was almost too much to bear.

"Laura," he murmured, stroking her hair.

She looked into his eyes, bit her lip. "I'm sorry I didn't tell you about the will."

"It's okay," he said, meaning it. "If you'd told me, I wouldn't still be here, and right now there's literally nowhere else I'd rather be." His voice was husky. He cleared his throat. "I have some vacation time saved up. I could probably stay a little longer."

She went completely still for a second. "Okay, Harvard," she whispered. "Then stay."

He leaned back to look at her. Her eyes were like liquid pools of light. "You want me here?"

She nodded, looking down, looking shy.

"Say it." He tilted her chin up. *"Please."*

He heard the desperation in his voice, and she must have heard it, too, because she gave him what he needed. "I want you here, Jonathan."

He kissed her again, joy welling up in the deepest place inside him. She wanted him to stay. She had feelings for him, too.

"You're so beautiful," he breathed, smoothing her dark, thick hair back from her eyes.

What he didn't say was the word that was playing on an endless repeat loop in his head:

Mine.

Chapter Fourteen

Wednesday morning dawned bright and unseasonably warm. Laura found Jonathan in the kitchen, cooking scrambled eggs.

He grinned at her. "Good morning, Gorgeous."

She beamed right back. After those sweet kisses in the kitchen yesterday evening, they'd both had some soup, then watched TV in the parlor while they waited for Chloe to bring Emma home. Laura had felt so happy sitting there next to him, his arm around her shoulders, like life was full of possibility in a way it hadn't been for a long time. She felt that way now, too—happy, extra alive.

He handed her a plate of eggs, still grinning, then dropped a quick kiss on her forehead. "What do you want to do today? Is Emma up?"

"She'll be down any second. And you're the tourist. What do *you* want to do?"

He ran a hand through his hair. "Whale watching, maybe? Or is it too early in the season for that?"

"It's better in the summer. Plus, trying to keep

Emma entertained for hours on a boat?" she said. "Not ideal."

He spooned some eggs onto his plate. "I hear there's a good children's museum in Boston…"

"And spend four hours with her in the car? I wouldn't inflict that on my worst enemy."

"We could turn it into an overnight trip," he said. "Two hours in the car today, two hours tomorrow. Go to the museum during the day and then I could take you to Fenway tonight. Hot dogs, popcorn, the whole shebang. Has Emma ever been to a game?"

A warning bell sounded in her head. "We don't have the money to stay at—"

"Don't worry about it. I'll get you girls a hotel room."

She bit her lip, feeling uneasy. "Jonathan…"

"Seriously. It would be fun. I'd like to show you where I live, take you around the neighborhood."

Laura studied him carefully. His eagerness was making her anxious. "I don't think that's a good idea."

"Why not? Maybe you'll like it. Maybe you'll want to come back."

"I lived in Boston most of my life. I know what it's like."

He put his arm around her, gave her a playful squeeze. "But you don't know what Boston's like with *me*."

It was too much. It was too soon. It was Conrad all over again. "We're *not* going to Boston today."

He sighed, dropped his arm. "Maybe over the weekend, then."

"Maybe." She heard the ambivalence in her voice, saw that he did, too.

He looked away. "Any museums closer to home that she likes?" His voice sounded strained.

She thought for a moment. "The Cape Cod Museum of Natural History in Brewster's pretty cool. She likes the stuffed birds and the nature trails. And sometimes they bring in therapy dogs and let the kids play with them."

He gave a crisp nod. "Sounds good. Let's do that."

They carried the plates into the dining room, where Emma was sitting with two of her stuffed animals, engrossed in a conversation with them.

"Hey, Tiny," Jonathan said. "Do your stuffed toys like scrambled eggs?"

Emma held up the two fake cats. "Kitties love eggs, Mr. Jonafin!" she said in an unnaturally high voice.

"Excellent." He set her plate down with a flourish. "Eat up, kitties. We've got a fun day ahead."

"Where are we going?" Emma asked, still serving as the voice of her stuffed cats.

"The natural history museum, honey," Laura said.

"To see the birdies?"

"And maybe the dogs."

"Yay!"

Jonathan sat and ate a forkful of eggs. "Does your mother want to come along?"

Laura doubted it. "We can ask."

They finished their breakfast and Laura went to find her mom. Eleanor didn't want to accompany them to the museum, so Laura decided to call Chloe and invite her along. Maybe if they brought a chaperone with them, Jonathan would put the brakes on a little and stop talking about spiriting her away to Boston.

She took her phone outside and sat on the steps of the back porch, her toes digging into the cold morning sand. After Chloe explained that she had some work to do at the restaurant that day, Laura said, "He kissed me last night, Chlo."

Chloe laughed. "So all it took to get you two crazy kids together was a near case of hypothermia, huh?"

"Am I crazy? I'm crazy, aren't I?"

"No, honey, you're *happy*. That's a good thing."

Odd—she'd felt happy earlier, but now she just felt anxious, thinking of how he'd wanted to take her and Emma to Boston. "You're the one who told me he could be an ax murderer!" she exclaimed.

"He came to church with you, sister," Chloe said gently. "I think I could be persuaded to change my opinion of him if you decide to keep him around."

"It's too fast, though, isn't it? I'm rushing into this just like I rushed into things with Conrad. And I've got Emma to think about now. I can't just start introducing her to strange men."

"Slow down there, cowgirl. First of all, Jonathan's already been here for a week and Emma loves him— he's hardly a stranger. Secondly, this Conrad stuff is baloney. You have to stop holding him up as the man against whom everyone else is measured."

The more Laura talked, though, the more she felt sure that things were moving too fast, spiraling out of control. "I just can't help thinking that Jonathan'll be the same. Comes on strong in the beginning, but then his true colors will start to emerge."

"Look, sweetie, I know Conrad did a number on you, but that's, like, hard-core cynical."

Laura bit her lip. Was it cynical—or realistic? Because, as all Jonathan's talk of Boston had reminded her, he was definitely leaving. He had the documents he needed. First he would leave, and then he'd take the inn away.

Jonathan watched Emma pat the therapy dog—a golden retriever in a navy blue vest—in the back garden of the Museum of Natural History, her little face ecstatic. The museum itself was small, but the garden out back was nicely landscaped, the butterfly house was a hit with Emma, and the nature trail behind it all was undeniably cool. He put his arm around Laura's shoulders, but once again, as she'd been doing all morning, she slipped away.

"Ever think about getting a dog?" he asked.

She tilted her head thoughtfully to the side. "She'd love it, wouldn't she?"

He could picture it so clearly. The woman, the girl, the dog, the beach. Throwing a stick into the ocean, the dog coming back to them happy and panting, spraying them all with water, dropping the stick at his feet. "She'd make you buy all kinds of little dog sweaters and shoes."

Laura looked up at him. "Did you really have a Chihuahua growing up?"

"My sister had a Chihuahua," he insisted. "It was *my sister's* dog."

"Uh-huh." She grinned at him. "Did you carry him around in a little purse?"

"She was a girl dog. And yeah, Charlotte had a

purse for her. And a tutu. And sweaters. And an Easter outfit with bunny ears."

"Bunny ears?"

"Bunny ears. It was hilarious. We wanted to take a family picture with her, but she couldn't stand the ears and kind of went crazy trying to get them off."

Laura gave a breathless laugh, a few wisps of hair falling out of her ponytail. She was so beautiful when she was happy. He wanted her to be happy all the time.

"Would you ever get another dog?" she asked.

"I like the big guys like this one," he said, pointing his chin toward Emma and the golden retriever. "A husky or a German shepherd or a Lab."

"You should get one."

He shook his head. "Apartment living isn't exactly where it's at for a big dog."

She shrugged. "You could move."

"I work on Boylston Street. My place is in Back Bay, right on the Charles River. It's pretty great to be able to walk to work."

"Riverfront, huh? Fancy."

In his mind's eye, he could see the brownstones lining the streets that weaved through his neighborhood, lines of English lampposts lighting the way at night. He liked his neighborhood, he did, but it was full of driven young professionals like him, with hardly a family in sight.

If she and Emma were to move to Boston, they'd probably want to find somewhere else to live.

"Where did you grow up?" he asked.

"Lexington."

He whistled. "Let me guess. A big Colonial?"

She nodded. "Yup."

"Did you get into the city much?"

"When I was at BU, I was in the city. My dorm was right next to Fenway Park. When I was little, my sisters and I went to a private school in Cambridge, so I've spent a lot of time there, too."

"I like Cambridge," he mused. He liked the bustle of Harvard Square. The Brattle Theatre with its artsy, indie films; the little cafés and hole-in-the-wall restaurants; the outstanding jazz club at the Charles Hotel. He hadn't been there much since law school—it seemed too far out of the way, somehow, too much effort and too much time away from work.

Was he *that* guy? Really? It wasn't even close to Christmas, but suddenly Jonathan was feeling a lot like the Grinch.

He turned to Laura, reached out and took her hand. "Have you ever been to the Regattabar Jazz Club?"

She shook her head, letting him hold her hand but not really holding his back.

"Want to go with me sometime?"

"Jonathan…" she said, biting her lip, her eyes cutting to where Emma was still patting the dog. "I thought we talked about this. Boston's too far for—"

"It's not that far. Just two hours. I want to take you out, Laura, on a proper date."

"In Boston," she said, her lips drawn tight.

"I know Boston. I don't know Wychmere Bay."

"It's just—" She stopped, looked at him. "What are we doing here, Jonathan?"

He felt his brow furrow. "What do you mean, what are we doing here?"

She gestured back and forth between them. "I mean, you, me. What is this?"

"I like you, Laura. I like you *a lot*." He wanted her to know that he was sincere, he was committed. Truly, he'd never felt like this before.

His words, though, did the opposite of what he'd intended. She looked away, nervous and maybe a little upset. "This isn't... I mean, I shouldn't—"

He was coming on too strong, he could feel it, but couldn't stop himself from pressing on. "I'm going to the hockey thing with Nate and Brett tonight, but can I take you out tomorrow, just you and me? Dinner, here in Wychmere Bay? Somewhere nice?"

She chewed her lip. "I don't know."

He could feel her slipping away and it made him desperate. "Friday, then? Or this weekend?"

"Jonathan..."

His jaw hardened. "Don't say it."

"You live in Boston," she said gently. "And I live on Cape Cod."

"It's not that far of a drive. And once you sell the inn, you'll be free to—"

"I'm sorry," she blurted out. "I think kissing you last night was a mistake."

"A mistake," he echoed, his voice flat.

"You and I, we want different things."

"Tell me what you want."

She shook her head. "It doesn't work that way."

"Why not? Why can't it work that way?" he pleaded. "If you tell me what you want, I'll give it to you. I swear, I'll give you anything you want."

"You want to make partner. It's what you've worked

for your entire life." The look in her eyes was kind. That made it worse.

"Yes, but—"

"Emma and I can't be with a man who's married to his job. We just can't."

He shook his head stubbornly. "We have a connection. Last night, when we kissed… I know you felt it, too."

She bit her lip again. Her voice wavered. "That was attraction, that's all."

He rocked back on his heels. She didn't feel it, then, this thing that had overtaken him. And if she didn't feel it, what more could he do?

"I don't think what we want is so different, but I get it," he said, resigned. "You don't like me the way I like you. It's okay."

She gave him a sharp, disbelieving look, and he did his best to give her a reassuring smile, even though it felt as if the core of him were crumbling. "Really," he reiterated. "It's okay."

"This thing with Carberry Hotels—"

"Laura," he said, taking her soft, smooth hand and clasping it in his own. "No hard feelings. Truly. If we end up working on it together in the fall, I can be professional about it. I promise."

She let out a small sigh of relief and he had to stop himself from sucking in a breath of pain. He was glad she felt better, glad that he'd been able to allay her concerns, but how he wished things could be different. How he wished she'd felt what he'd felt when they'd kissed. The same sense of devotion, the same—dare he say it, even to himself?—depths of love.

Chapter Fifteen

Laura watched Jonathan's profile as he drove the car. Emma was singing "Yankee Doodle" for the millionth time in the back seat. He'd moved her car seat into his BMW before they'd left, despite Laura's protests that it might rough up his leather seats.

"Bet you'll be happy to have a break from 'Yankee Doodle' for a while," she said, grasping at anything to say that might end the awkward silence between them. Why had she thought it would be a good idea to break up with him at the museum, when they still had to endure all this time together in the car?

Was it really a breakup, though? They hadn't really been together, had they? A couple of impulsive kisses didn't equate to a relationship, did they?

If only she'd stopped him before he'd kissed her…

Because he'd been right in saying that they had a connection, despite what she'd said to him back at the museum. She'd seen the hurt that had rocked through him when she'd downplayed what was between them as mere attraction, and it had almost, *almost*, made her put her hand on his cheek and tell him that he was right, they had something rare and special, but she just couldn't turn her mind off and let her feelings carry her away.

Because her feelings couldn't be trusted. Hadn't she already proved that to herself with Conrad, and with Jonathan, even, coming home to find him in the parlor *with her mother*, laughing about the deal that was going to take the inn away from her?

Besides, what good would it do her to fall in love with a man who lived in Boston? She didn't want her daughter having the same kind of childhood she'd had—lots of material advantages but little real love.

And while she recognized, on some level, that it might be more the *idea* of Boston than the actual *place* that bothered her, she also knew that it wasn't just where he lived that was the problem. He was an ambitious man with a big job. Even if he did have feelings for her, he'd never have the time or attention to be the kind of partner she craved.

She remembered the day she and Conrad had decided to get married. They'd been dating about six months, and he was coming up on his law school graduation. "If I get a job in New York, will you come with me?" he'd asked. They'd been having dinner at some Thai restaurant in Brighton.

She'd been a college sophomore. Her friends had thought Conrad—with his blue eyes and his muscular build—was as suave as they came.

Conrad—who'd grown up wealthy like her, and reveled in it. Conrad—who'd parlayed his father's connections into acceptance at law school, and then traded on them again for a job offer in what he perceived as the center of the universe: New York City.

"Conrad, I can't just leave school—"

"If you loved me, you'd come. Do you love me, Laura?"

"Of course I do, but—"

He'd looked away from her, blue eyes flashing with irritation. "There's lots of girls who'd be excited to come to New York with me."

"It's not that I don't want to come, it's just—what would I do for work? I don't even have my degree yet. I don't know what I'd do."

"You wouldn't have to do anything."

She laughed. "Yeah, right. Because my dad would be *thrilled* to set me up in my own apartment in New York City where I could sit around and do *nothing* all day."

Now he looked really irritated. "Who said anything about your dad?"

"How else would I be able to afford New York?"

"Move in with me."

Laura almost choked on a bite of her red curry chicken. "Conrad, we're not even married. I just can't…"

He ran a hand through his light brown hair. "Fine. We'll do it your way. Marry me."

"What?"

He got down on one knee. A murmur ran through the restaurant. "I don't have a ring for you yet, but maybe you'll move to New York with your husband."

"Conrad," she said sharply. "You don't have to—"

"Apparently I do. So, what'll it be, Laura? Will you marry me or not?"

Her heart had been pounding—with hope, she'd told herself back then, but now she knew that it had been panic, pure and simple. Her heart had been pounding in panic, and she'd said yes because she'd been afraid that if she didn't—ready or not—she'd lose him.

She remembered telling her parents that she and Conrad were getting married at city hall in five days. Her mother had been upset that there would be no big wedding, but her father had been the one to ask if she was sure about this—certain that Conrad was the man who'd make her happy for the long haul.

She'd been angry with her father then, for having the nerve to talk to her about her happiness after abandoning her for his job in Hong Kong. She'd also been angry that he'd introduced doubt into her mind, although she recognized now that he hadn't so much introduced it as called it to the fore.

She remembered walking into the courthouse in her off-the-rack dress, her grandmother her matron of honor, Conrad's roommate the best man. He'd bought her a cheap sterling silver bridal ring set with a princess-cut cubic zirconia center stone and a row of tiny round CZ stones set around the sides of the band. He'd told her he'd buy her a real diamond after he started his new job, although he never had.

Even at their small, celebratory dinner at a seafood restaurant in Faneuil Hall, she'd felt inexplicably sad. She'd thought to herself, *This is new, this is strange, this is different, that's all. You'll feel better about things in the morning. It's just a case of the post-wedding blues.*

She hadn't felt better in the morning. But her girlfriends had all been a little envious and in awe about the fact that she was married, and she hadn't had the heart to tell anyone that she thought she might have made a mistake.

And then, barely a month later, she'd gotten pregnant, and that was that. No more room for doubts—at least not for her.

She snuck another glance at Jonathan. His hands tightened on the steering wheel in response to her question about getting sick of hearing "Yankee Doodle." "I don't mind her singing." He gave her a small smile, but it didn't reach his eyes. "I kind of like it, actually."

She didn't know how to reply. There was a part of her—a large part of her—that didn't want things with him to end this way, but whom was she kidding? Eventually, even if he didn't feel that way now, she'd just be someone who was keeping him from staying focused on his career.

Someone to be pampered and put aside, like her mother.

Or cheated on and discarded, like her.

They got off the highway and passed a three-hundred-year-old cemetery in the back of a small white church. Laura stared out the window, not looking at him. Very carefully not looking at the way his hair—without gel—almost reached his eyes. "You can stay, you know, if you want to take a vacation."

"I'm leaving in the morning," he said.

She felt something dark and clawing squeeze her chest. "All right," she said quietly, keeping her face turned away from him, not knowing what else to say.

"I had a nice time here, with you. And Emma." His

words were muted, and although she wasn't looking at him, she could tell he'd taken his eyes off the road to look at her.

"I'm glad," she murmured. He seemed sincere, but she couldn't chance it. Not with Emma to think about. She had to guard not only her own heart, but her daughter's heart, as well.

They pulled up to the inn and got out of the car. It had gotten windy, and the sound of the waves hitting the shore was loud, even from this far away.

He pointed toward the beach. "I'm going to go for a walk."

"Mr. Jonafin, the water's too cold for swimming!" Emma chirped.

He laughed and ruffled her hair, though his eyes were sad. "Don't worry, Tiny. I learned my lesson. I won't go in again."

Laura felt a familiar sense of panic well up inside her, and she almost stopped him. *Don't leave.* But the last time she'd let that panic take the lead in her life, she'd ended up at the courthouse with Conrad and his CZ ring and his indifference.

She couldn't—*wouldn't*—risk that again.

Jonathan's gaze moved from Emma to Laura. "See you later," he said quietly.

"See you later," she echoed softly, confused about why it hurt so much to say goodbye.

Pastor Nate and his ten-year-old son, Hayden, lived in a small cedar-shingled cottage next to the church. The kitchen had clearly been updated and was open to the living room, which housed a huge flat-screen and a leather sectional that looked comfortably worn in.

"Hey, Jonathan! Glad you could make it!" Nate greeted him, taking the six-pack of root beer Jonathan had brought with him. "Meet my son, Hayden. Hayden, this is Jonathan. He's been staying at The Sea Glass Inn."

"Hello, sir," the boy said, extending his hand.

"Call me Jonathan."

The boy grinned. He wore glasses like his dad. "All right. Jonathan it is."

"Come on in." Nate clamped a hand on his shoulder. "Game's about to begin."

"Thanks." Jonathan nodded at the men milling around the living room, most of whom he recognized from the church service on Sunday.

Brett was standing at the kitchen table, wearing a Bruins jersey, eating tortilla chips and guacamole like they were going out of style. "Dude," he called, motioning Jonathan over. "You eaten yet?"

Jonathan shook his head. Since his conversation with Laura that afternoon, he hadn't had much of an appetite.

"Try the wings."

Jonathan picked up a paper plate and helped himself to a couple. They were good, hot and tangy, although they did nothing to expel the feeling of emptiness that had lodged itself in his chest.

"Wanna know the secret?" Brett asked, grinning. "Worcestershire sauce. That stuff is *gold*."

"Nice." Jonathan set down his plate.

"Pizza should be getting here any second."

"I'm not that hungry."

Brett shrugged. "All the more for me."

Jonathan watched Hayden grab an orange soda out of the fridge and plant himself on the couch. "I didn't know Nate had a kid."

"Sad story." Brett glanced around and lowered his voice. "His wife's appendix burst when she was eight months pregnant. Died on the operating table. Never met her son."

Jonathan sucked in a breath. "That's brutal."

"Tell me about it, man."

Brett filled his plate with more chips. "Hey, I heard about what you did for Ethan Malone. That was solid, brother. I don't know what he was doing with that stupid fake ID, but I promise you, he's a good kid."

"Yeah, I got that sense when I met with him. I hope the diversion program works out for him. It would be a shame for him to have an arrest record following him around for the rest of his life."

Brett eyed him carefully. "Seems like working with kids is right up your alley. How'd you end up in corporate law?"

Jonathan frowned. Working with kids was right up his alley? Where had Brett come up with that? Before last weekend, he'd never worked with kids a day in his life.

And how *had* he ended up in corporate law? As far back as he could remember, that had always been his goal, but he couldn't really remember why. There was the money and the prestige, but he couldn't deny that the thought of continuing to work and work and work just to amp up his ego suddenly left him feeling…empty. Cold.

"I don't know, man," he told Brett. "I honestly can't remember. And ever since I got here, I've felt unsettled, like everything's upside down."

"I felt the same way after my parents died. It shook everything up."

Jonathan felt a flash of recognition. "Yeah, it's like I'm questioning my entire life, and I'm finding it kind of…lacking. Like this path I've been on for so long just isn't right."

"I've been there, man. Change. It's rough, isn't it?"

"Yes!" Jonathan was relieved Brett didn't think he was crazy.

"Right," Brett said, "so this is the point where a lot of people get scared and turn back. They think change can't be worth it if it's causing them pain. So, they give up. They shut down. They ignore God's call and cling to whatever it was that was giving them self-worth or self-esteem in the first place—money, power, whatever. They don't want to let it go.

"So, I guess the question you've gotta ask yourself is whether or not that old life's gonna keep you satisfied now that you've heard that call. Do you want to go back and pretend you didn't hear it? Or do you have the courage to become a man after God's own heart?"

Jonathan blew out a long breath. "Dude, that's heavy."

Brett laughed. "Tell me about it!"

A few of the guys on the couch called them over for the national anthem on TV. The Bruins won the face-off and took off down the ice with the puck. Jonathan watched but his mind was churning. After a minute he turned to Brett and, in a low voice, said, "I don't think I can do it. Pretend I didn't hear it, I mean."

Brett smiled and swatted him on the knee. "I couldn't, either, brother."

"Is it worth it?"

Brett's smile grew bigger. "Yeah, it's worth it. It's hard sometimes, but it's worth it. A hundred percent."

They turned their attention back to the game, which was a close one, the Bruins edging out the Leafs by an overtime goal.

After the game, Brett and Jonathan went to the pizza parlor on Main Street to see who was better at pinball. Brett was competitive and they played for over an hour. It felt good to be distracted from Laura's rejection. It felt good to be distracted from his second thoughts about his career. It also felt like, after so many years of going it alone, he finally had a real friend.

"So, I don't know what your plans are, but if you wanna come back down and see a certain someone on the weekends and maybe help out with the ball hockey practice again, you're more than welcome to crash at my place," Brett said.

Jonathan shook his head. It was agony to think about her—kissing her, holding her, hearing her say it was a mistake. "Thanks, but she doesn't want me here."

Brett raised an eyebrow, looking away from the pinball machine as the ball flipped back and forth along the bumpers at the top. "Um, you do realize my sister, Chloe, is her best friend, right? I hear all their female chitter-chatter."

"She told me. Point-blank. This afternoon. I told

her I have feelings for her and she said that getting involved with me was a mistake."

Brett winced. "Sorry, man."

Jonathan raked a hand through his hair. "I think I moved too fast. She said we're looking for different things."

"I've known Laura for a long time," Brett said slowly, "and I don't know about that."

"No?"

Brett fed another quarter into the pinball machine. "Stay the course, brother. I have a feeling she'll probably come around."

Chapter Sixteen

Laura woke up to insistent knocking on her door. She rolled over, sticking her pillow over her head, confident that whoever was knocking, it wasn't Emma, who had access to her room through the adjoining door.

She hadn't slept well at all last night. She'd been having weird dreams about Gram and her wedding to Conrad…except it hadn't been Conrad she'd been marrying in her dream, it had been Jonathan, and instead of cubic zirconia, he'd given her a huge diamond ring.

"Get up, Laura. Get up now!" her mother called through the door.

A spike of adrenaline shot through her. Was it Emma? Had something happened?

She leaped out of bed and pulled the door to the hallway open. "What's wrong? What's going on?"

Although it was barely seven o'clock in the morning, her mother was dressed to kill in a Chanel suit, heels and makeup that even a model would envy. "I'm leaving, darling. Daddy needs me."

Laura's mind immediately leaped to a series of

worst-case scenarios: heart attack, cancer, car accident on one of Hong Kong's steep, winding roads. "What happened? Is Dad okay?"

"There's a business junket in Dubai, and all the clients' wives are going. Your father needs me to keep them entertained."

Laura's mouth dropped open. "What? Are you kidding me right now?"

"I know you wanted me to stay for the summer, but I can't. I'm sorry. Some things are more important than this dusty old inn."

"But what about Carberry Hotels?"

Her mother sniffed. "That was all for you, darling. Daddy and I don't need the money. But if you don't want it… I need to get back to my real life."

"The *money* isn't important to me, Mom, but the inn—" Laura stopped, took a breath. "You know this isn't what Gram would have wanted."

"Your grandmother's gone," her mother said. "It doesn't matter what she wanted."

"It matters to me," Laura said quietly.

Her mother sniffed again, touched her hair. "I don't know what to tell you, darling. Maybe if you were still married, you'd understand. But when your father needs me, he *needs* me. I'm not going to turn my back on him for this old place."

Okay, she could understand that. Almost involuntarily, she glanced down the hall at the door to Jonathan's room. "Have you told Jonathan yet?"

"Yes, darling. I told him. He'd just come back in from a run."

Laura helped her mother carry her giant suitcase

down the stairs. Jonathan came down a few minutes later, dressed in a suit, his own suitcase in hand. "Eleanor," he said, pure business. "You're headed out?"

Laura's mother gave him her hand for one of those limp, fingertip-only handshakes. "Sorry we sent you on a wild-goose chase."

"I'll talk to Nate before I go," he said. "You never know, the church might want to sell."

Laura felt her stomach drop. He was leaving—he was really leaving.

The inn, the deal—that was what mattered to him. Not her, not Emma—his deal.

He offered to help Eleanor take her suitcase to her car, but her mother had ordered a town car that hadn't yet arrived.

Now that she was of no use to him on his deal, Laura half expected him to extend his hand to her in a businesslike manner, too, to brush her off with an easy compliment and a quick goodbye, but he surprised her. "Laura, can I talk to you for a second outside?"

She followed him onto the back patio, the air cool, the dunes empty, the sound of the waves hitting the shore loud and hypnotic.

"I don't want to leave like this," he said. His eyes were dark and pleading.

Then don't.

Instead of saying it, though, she stared at him, intentionally playing dumb. Everybody left her. If it wasn't now, it would be only a matter of time. "Like what?"

He ran a hand through his hair. His tie was red, the

same one from the night they'd met. "I need you to know, my feelings for you—I don't take them lightly."

She kept quiet, waiting to hear what else it was he had to say.

"I don't just like you, Laura. I'm falling in love with you."

She let out a gasp, took a step away. "Don't," she said. "You can't say that to me as you're walking out the door."

"Tell me to come back and I will. I'll come back tonight."

"And then what? Wait for the next time you leave?"

"We can figure this out. Please. Give me a chance. Give *us* a chance." His eyes were begging her to give their relationship a chance.

He stepped toward her but she backed away, shaking her head. "There is no *us*, Jonathan."

"You don't mean that."

"Don't tell me how I feel!" She crossed her arms over her chest. "You and Conrad, you're exactly the same."

"Is that his name? Your ex? Conrad?"

She clenched her jaw, looked away.

"I'm not him, sweetheart," he said, his voice gentle. "I'm not here to hurt you."

"Well, what do you think's going to happen, Harvard? He used my feelings for him to get me to do what he wanted me to do," she said, thinking about Jonathan and Boston, Conrad and New York. "Tell me you're not trying to do the exact same thing."

He reared back as though she'd slapped him. "I'm

not trying to get you to do anything except give this thing between us a chance."

"I told you already," she said, turning away, her voice intentionally cold, intentionally dismissive, "there's nothing between us except chemistry. At least not on my end."

There was a long moment of silence, and Laura was tempted to look back at him, but she resisted the urge. If she looked at him now, she'd cave, and she couldn't. She couldn't. She had to be strong. For her. For Emma. She had to prove to herself that she wasn't going to get tricked into loving someone who didn't love her back ever again.

"Okay," Jonathan said finally, his voice defeated. "I had to try." After another long moment of silence, he added, "Tell Emma I said goodbye, will you?"

She nodded, her back still turned toward him, not trusting herself to reply out loud.

She heard the sliding glass door into the parlor slide open, then slide closed. She sat heavily on the steps of the patio, watching the light at the end of the jetty blink on and off, off and on.

I'm falling in love with you, he'd said.

And then he'd left anyway, to see if he could salvage his partnership by talking to Pastor Nate.

She was crying, and she was angry about it. Why had she been stupid enough to let herself care about him? She'd known what would happen. She'd always known that his career would win out in the end.

I'm falling in love with you.

The patio door opened again and she turned before

she could stop herself, but it wasn't Jonathan. It was her mother, looking thoughtful.

Laura sat up straighter, wiped the tears from her face. "Is he gone?"

Her mother nodded. "He's gone."

"Good."

Her mother rested an awkward hand on Laura's shoulder. "You know, darling, all your father and I ever wanted for you was to be happy."

Laura snorted. "Can we please not do this now?"

"I know you blame me and your father for what happened with Conrad, and maybe I should have made my objections more clear—"

"What objections, Mom? You wanted me to get married at the country club! With a big, frilly dress!"

"Yes," her mother said, "because when you commit your life to someone, darling, you shouldn't do it quietly and then slink away into the night as though you're ashamed. The fact that you two didn't *want* any fanfare was worrisome."

Laura pressed her lips into a thin line.

Her mother touched Laura's cheek. "What I said the other day about your father being proud of you was true. We've always been proud of you, darling, and that didn't change with your divorce."

Laura closed her eyes, trying to work it through, but the pieces wouldn't click into place. Because they'd sent her away. She remembered the shame of being left behind, the sense of crippling unworthiness, the feeling that, no matter what she did, she would never be enough.

"I always felt like a disappointment to you."

Her mother laughed, a strangled noise that sounded like it was full of glass. "Oh, darling. Would you believe I never felt good enough for *you*?"

Her mother's phone chirped, and she looked at the screen. "That's my driver," Eleanor said, getting to her feet. "Take care of yourself, darling." Laura stood and her mother leaned in to air-kiss both of Laura's cheeks.

"You, too, Mom."

And as she watched her mother teeter away in her designer clothes and her heels, Laura realized that she wasn't even angry that her mother was leaving. She was sad about losing the inn, but at least she knew that, in her own way, her mother loved her.

Maybe instead of focusing on everything that had happened in the past, she could simply choose to look forward. Forgive her parents—and Conrad, even—for what they hadn't been able to give her and find the people who could give her what she needed today.

Her mother's words echoed in her head: *When your father needs me, he* needs *me, darling. I'm not going to turn my back on him for this old place.*

The place, the person. The person, the place. Maybe her mother's leaving was a blessing in disguise. She'd wanted to keep the inn to keep her grandmother's legacy alive, but her mother was right—Gram was gone. She wasn't coming back. But Jonathan...

Jonathan was here, and he was falling in love with her, and she'd shoved him out the door.

She'd been so busy comparing him to Conrad and her father, right from the start, and for what?

To protect herself.

Because he was a thousand times the man Conrad

had been, and she'd been terrified that if she fell in love with him, he wouldn't love her back. So terrified, it seemed, that when he'd handed her his heart on a platter, she'd knocked it to the ground and crushed it under her feet.

What had she been *thinking*?

She loved him. She needed him. If she and Emma had to move, if he had to work more than she might like... Well, he was right—they could figure it out.

She didn't care if she had to go to Boston or Hong Kong or New York. She had to get him back.

Jonathan collapsed into a chair at the Cape Cod Coffee Co. on Main Street and put his face in his hands. He'd wanted Brett to be right about Laura so badly. He'd hoped—man, how he'd hoped—that by telling her how he felt, he could change her mind about saying goodbye.

But he hadn't convinced her. She hadn't changed her mind. And now he had to go back to Boston without her *or* the deal that could have saved his career.

And... He didn't want to leave. He liked this town, he liked these people, but most of all, he liked *himself* when he was here, and he just, really did not want to go.

"Can I get you anything?" a teenage barista asked him, hovering by the side of his table. The girl had blond hair and braces, her sunny disposition a perfect match to the shop, which was bright and airy, with wooden tables, wooden chairs and a variety of colorful surfboards mounted on the walls.

"Just coffee," he said. "Black."

The girl nodded, but she was looking at him strangely, as though she knew him from somewhere, but couldn't quite figure it out. He took out his phone, hoping she'd take it as a cue to stop staring, but instead she said, "Um, you're that guy, aren't you? The one who helped Ethan Malone?"

He put his phone down and looked at her warily. He 100 percent did not want to be the guy people came to for free legal advice. "Yeah, that was me."

She crumpled into the chair across from him. "I'm his girlfriend. Talia Morgan. I can't even tell you… Just, thank you so much, sir."

"Uh, you're welcome."

"It was so stupid," she said. "A bunch of us were hanging out, and everyone always razzes Ethan that he looks just like Drew's older brother, and we thought it would be funny to, like, dare him to take Drew's brother's ID and see if he could use it. We weren't even drinking and we didn't actually *want* alcohol, we just wanted to see if he could, like, do it, you know? It was so dumb."

Jonathan folded his hands on the table. "Yeah, doesn't sound like the smartest idea."

"I was so freaked he was gonna actually, like, have to go to prison or something. And, then, when we heard you got him that deal, it was just, like, such a relief."

"I can imagine," he said mildly, "but he's not out of the woods just yet. The Juvenile Diversion Program still has to make a determination about whether or not to accept him."

"They will, though. I know they will, sir. And

you're, like, his hero now. We're going to UMass together in the fall, and we don't have to declare our majors until sophomore year or whatever, but he's already totally decided that he's going to do prelaw."

"Well, I'm glad he's got plans for the future," Jonathan said, at a loss for how else to respond.

The girl stood up. "Do you, like, want a doughnut or anything with your coffee? My treat, totally."

"I'm good, Talia. But thanks."

"Okay, but the coffee's on me, sir. Because you're awesome. So, like, thanks again." She gave him a thumbs-up and in return he gave her an awkward little two-finger salute.

"You can call me Jonathan."

"Jonathan," she gushed. "That's so cool of you. I always thought lawyers were kind of stuffy or whatever, but you're, like, totally cool."

She walked backward for a couple of steps, grinning at him like a lunatic, until she bumped into another table and turned away with an embarrassed "Okay, then" and a wave.

He ducked his head and shook it, smiling. Teenagers were funny creatures.

Who did stupid things.

And often needed help.

He picked his phone up and typed *juvenile law* into the search bar. Then he started to read.

Two hours later, Jonathan still hadn't moved from his table at the coffee shop. He'd been researching and making phone calls. The positions he was looking at paid crumbs compared with his current job, but his career had never really been about money for him—it had always been some combination of self-protection and perfectionism and prestige.

He kept thinking about what Brett had said last night: *the question you've gotta ask yourself is whether or not that old life's gonna keep you satisfied now that you've heard that call. Do you want to go back and pretend you didn't hear it? Or do you have the courage to become a man after God's own heart?*

He picked up his phone again. He knew this might seem sudden, or out of the blue, to his colleagues, but the truth was he'd been feeling dissatisfied with his career for a long time now—if he'd ever really been satisfied with it at all.

Mike Roe picked up on the first ring. "J-Man," he said. "What's the word? You must have got that deal wrapped up nice and tight, huh, because I just got off the phone with the CEO of Carberry Hotels."

"Uh…no, actually. The deal's not going to happen. At least not until the fall," Jonathan said, wondering what the church would do with the inn come September.

"Huh. Weird. Well, Carberry seemed very interested in retaining our services anyway, so whatever you did to convince them, well done."

Jonathan scratched his head. Connor must have pulled through for him and put in a good word with his father, despite being upset that Jonathan hadn't been able to get the job done. That was a first—someone who was so predictably unpredictable actually following through on his word.

"So, if the deal's off the table," Mike said, "when can I expect you back?"

"Actually," Jonathan said, taking a sip of his now-cold coffee, "that's what I wanted to talk to you about. I've been rethinking a few things, and I'm not so sure I want to come back at all."

"Aw, come on, not you, too," his mentor replied. "Don't tell me. You want to join a Buddhist monastery? Travel around the world? Cure cancer? Save the trees?"

Jonathan laughed. "No, nothing like that."

"So, what is it? You've been here long enough to know that if you leave, you're not coming back."

Jonathan nodded. He knew.

He'd always thought that those who left were weak and just couldn't hack it. Now he could see that for a lot of them, it had probably been more a case of mismatched desires.

"Just time for a change," he said lightly.

"Is this about what I said to you about making partner?" Mike asked. "Because we can work something out."

Jonathan blinked. This wasn't the reaction he'd been expecting. He'd figured that after Mike had told him he was a dime a dozen, he'd be happy enough to show him the door. "I appreciate that, and I value everything you've done for me, Mike, but I just don't see myself staying at the firm long term."

"Take some time and sleep on it, Masters. I don't want you doing anything you can't take back."

Jonathan glanced around the coffee shop, which was pretty much empty now, then out the window at

Wychmere Bay—its modesty, its charm. If becoming a partner didn't hinge on bringing in new business, if he didn't have to make a desperate final bid to close The Sea Glass Inn deal by any means necessary, did that change how he felt about staying on at the firm? Was now really the time to go?

"Honestly, Mike," he said, "I've pretty much made up my mind."

"You got something else lined up?" his mentor asked.

"Not yet."

"Then take some time and sleep on it," Mike said again. "You've got a bunch of unused vacation time, don't you?"

"I do," Jonathan said slowly. Using his vacation time would at least give him the opportunity to explore his alternatives in greater detail. Maybe he could even impose on Brett's offer of hospitality, and stick around here for a while.

"You do good work," Mike said. "I'd like to keep you around."

"Well, gee," Jonathan replied, knowing exactly what to say to keep Mike happy, "don't get all mushy on me."

Mike let out a bark of laughter. "What can I say? I'm a good friend—and don't you forget it!"

Chapter Seventeen

Jonathan left the coffee shop after talking to Brett about moving in for a few weeks and walked to the sandwich shop on the corner. He ordered a turkey club and took it outside, where there were a few sidewalk tables.

He felt good about his plan to stick around Wychmere Bay. Laura had said there was nothing between them but chemistry, but she'd also said she couldn't be with a man who was married to his job. Maybe when she saw that he was taking steps to disentangle himself from the law firm, she'd give him another chance.

He wouldn't be a stalker about it, but he loved her. He'd seen her eyes when he'd told her he was falling in love with her, and it hadn't been indifference he'd seen there, but fear.

And no wonder, with that deadbeat ex-husband of hers, and parents who'd left her to fend for herself while they'd jetted off to Hong Kong.

He could show her he was patient. He could show

her he was trustworthy. He could be there for her, to whatever degree she was willing to let him in.

Because while the reality of romantic love might be new to him, he understood that love wasn't about what you got out of it, but rather what you put in. She was everything he'd ever wanted, and he was willing to give her whatever she needed in return—time, space, stability, support.

He'd give her anything. He'd give her everything. If she'd just give him one more chance.

"Deep thoughts, young man?"

Jonathan looked up. Irene Perkins was grinning down at him, a box of fudge in her hands.

He stood to greet her. "Hello, Irene. Nice to see you again."

"Mind if I join you?"

"Of course not." He pulled out a chair for her. "Please."

She opened the box of fudge and nudged it toward him. "You look like you could use some of this."

He took a piece and popped it in his mouth. Chocolate Raspberry. It was ridiculously good.

"I heard Eleanor left this morning," she said.

He swallowed his fudge, nodded. "News travels fast."

"And you? Are you leaving, too?"

He shook his head. "No, not yet."

She patted his hand. "Good."

His phone rang. It was sitting faceup on the table, and he could see that the caller had a Cape Cod area code. His heart leaped. Was it Laura? They'd never exchanged cell numbers—why would they need to, when they were both staying at the inn?

"I'm sorry, Irene, I don't mean to be rude—"

"Take it, honey. Go ahead."

Jonathan picked up the phone. It wasn't Laura. It was Dean, from the Beacon Light Mission.

He had bad news about Jonathan's dad.

Laura made it to Boston in record time. Chloe had agreed to pick up Emma from preschool and keep her entertained for the afternoon so that Laura could track Jonathan down at Meyers, Suben & Roe.

The law firm was located in a high-rise on Boylston Street, a block or so down from the Prudential Center mall, right in the center of the city's action. Strangely enough, it was the huge stone facade of the Boston Public Library, dubbed a "palace for the people" by its architect, that always captured Laura's attention.

She used to study here on occasion when she was at Boston University, and she'd always found it soothing—the grand staircase with its murals, its stone lions, its arched windows and their filtered light. She'd spent many an hour in the Bates reading room, with its barrel-vaulted ceiling, endless book-cases and green reading lanterns spaced evenly on the long oak tables. The quiet in that room was pur-poseful, peaceful.

She tried to channel that feeling of peace and pur-pose, because now that she was here, she felt panicky again. What if he didn't want to see her? What if she'd misunderstood him? What if she was too late?

She parked in the ridiculously expensive lot beneath

Jonathan's office building and took the elevator up to his floor.

She checked in with the receptionist, who fetched her a bottle of sparkling water and asked her to sit on the hard leather couch opposite the reception desk to wait.

After a few minutes, the receptionist beckoned her back to the desk. "I'm afraid Mr. Masters isn't in the office today, Ms. Lessoway. He's on sabbatical for the next few weeks. I'm sorry."

"But… He was coming back today. I don't understand."

The receptionist smiled sympathetically. She was pretty and polished. She wore her headset like a crown. "Would you like to leave a message?"

"No," Laura said, feeling deflated. Then, in a last-ditch attempt, she asked, "Do you have his personal number? Or his address?"

The receptionist's smile hardened. "I'm sorry, but we don't give out that information."

"Oh. Of course not."

Laura walked out of the office. Where was he? Why hadn't they exchanged numbers? Why had he believed her when she'd said there was nothing between them except chemistry? Why hadn't he known that she was falling in love with him, too?

Her phone rang as she got onto the elevator. It was Chloe, who'd just spoken with Irene Perkins. She had bad news about Jonathan's dad.

Chapter Eighteen

Jonathan didn't like hospitals. He didn't like the fluorescent lighting, the laminated floors or the constant beeping. He didn't like the lack of privacy, the flimsy curtains separating the beds, the drafty hallways, the doors that never closed.

He'd been hospitalized once at six or seven years old when he'd had a nasty bout of salmonella poisoning, and he remembered how hard it had been for the nurse to find a vein for his IV. He'd kicked and screamed so much that they'd had to call in a couple of orderlies to hold him down. He remembered his mom standing in the corner, watching, a smile on her face that was meant to be comforting but was anything but.

His primary exposure to hospitals, though, was the hospital in Rochester where his father had ended up so many times during his childhood. He remembered the maroon-carpeted waiting room with its boxy TV, the volume never turned up loud enough to entirely mute the noise from the intake assessments being performed by the social workers. After a while, perhaps by his father's fifth or sixth admission, Jonathan had been able to distinguish between the families of the first-timers and those of the frequent-flyers—it was the difference between extreme anxiety and defeat.

Cape Cod Memorial Hospital, at least, was open and accessible. Visitors didn't have to sign a log or wait for visiting hours, and they didn't have to stay off the ward in a white-walled visiting room with orderlies who led in the patients and then stood watchfully by the door.

After ascertaining which room his father was in, Jonathan sprinted up the stairs to the third floor. He was still in his suit and tie and his shoes were smooth and a touch slippery, but he preferred the stairs to being trapped in a hospital elevator. He'd already been trapped in his car for what had felt like a never-ending, white-knuckled drive.

His father had been staying in one of the home-less camps in the woods. This morning, his friends had been unable to wake him. They'd had to call 911.

He skidded to a halt outside the door to the ICU. He pressed the buzzer. A nurse buzzed him in.

The nurse walked him to his father's bedside, told him the doctor would be there shortly. He'd spoken with a doctor on the phone before he'd gotten behind the wheel to drive here, a doctor who'd said things like "untreated, late-stage pancreatic cancer," "renal fail-ure" and "prepare yourself for the worst."

He'd been hoping that maybe there'd been a misun-derstanding, a case of mistaken identity—even iden-tity fraud.

There'd been no misunderstanding. The man unconscious in the bed looked old and haggard and dirty, but it was him—it was his dad.

Jonathan sat in the chair beside the bed, put his hand on top of his father's blanket. "Dad," he whispered. "Dad, it's Jonathan. I'm here."

He was hoping for a twitch, a movement, a sign that maybe his father knew he was there. He didn't get one. He dropped his head.

"Dad," he said, "I'm sorry I didn't try to find you sooner. I could never understand why you wouldn't just take the medication. It felt like you didn't care enough about us to accept long-term help." His voice cracked and he hated how broken he sounded, like a twelve-year-old kid instead of a thirty-two-year-old man.

He took a breath to steady himself, went on, "But that wasn't it, was it, Dad? You cared about us, didn't you? You cared about us, but you were just sick."

He cleared his throat. He was staring at his father's hand where it rested on top of the blanket. "Anyway, I just wanted you to know that I missed you. As much as we butted heads before you left, I missed you when you were gone."

He took his dad's hand and now he *did* feel a twitch. A jerk. A squeeze.

He looked at his dad's face. His eyes were open. "Jonathan?" his father whispered.

Jonathan leaned forward. He held his father's hand tighter. His heart was beating very fast. "It's me, Dad. I'm here."

"Are you real?"

"I'm real, Dad. I'm here."

"You're all grown-up."

Jonathan nodded, not trusting himself to speak.

"You're a good son," his father rasped. "You always were. Will you—" He coughed, a long, hacking cough that sounded painful. "Will you tell your mother I'm sorry? For everything?"

"I'll tell her," Jonathan said. There was a terrible pressure behind his eyes, a heaviness, a weight. He'd wanted to find his father so he could help him, not so he could say goodbye.

"And your sister—tell her I'm sorry, too."

"I'll tell her, Dad. I love you. We all love you." He was clutching his father's hand.

His father's eyes fixed on a point over Jonathan's shoulder. "Oh, look!" he said, and his face lit up. "Look!"

Jonathan glanced over his shoulder, but there was nothing there. When he turned back to the bed, his father was gone.

Laura stopped in the doorway. She saw the man in the bed lying still, the monitors beside him dark and quiet. She saw the man sitting next to the bed, his back hunched, his face in his hands.

"Oh, Jonathan, no!" She ran to him, and then, somehow, she was in his lap.

"I'm sorry," she whispered, stroking his hair, her face pressed up against his neck, wetting it with her tears. "I'm so sorry."

And then he was crying, too, and holding her, his grief washing over her in a torrent that felt like it would never end.

Finally, a long time later, he drew back from her. "Laura," he croaked. "What are you doing here?"

She touched his face. She had to touch his face. "Chloe called me. She said Irene was with you when… when you got the call."

He nodded, studying her.

"I would have been here sooner," she said, "but I was in Boston when she called."

Confusion flickered across his face. "You were in Boston? Why?"

She rested her forehead against his temple. "I went to your office. To find you."

She felt his breathing speed up, felt the rise and fall of his chest get faster. "You went to Boston to find me," he repeated.

She nodded. She pressed her nose into his cheek.

"Why?" he said again.

She took a deep breath and straightened up so she could look him in the eye. "Because when you left this morning, you told me you were falling in love with me, and I didn't say it back."

His hands, where they were holding her, gave a little tremor. "And did you want to say it back?" His eyes were dark and urgent and searching, and she could tell she had the power to break him with a word.

"Yes," she breathed, laying her palm on his cheek. He closed his eyes and pressed his face into her hand. "I love you, Jonathan. I'm sorry I wasn't there when you got the phone call, but I'm here now."

"You're here now," he murmured, a note of wonder creeping in, "and you love me."

"Yeah, Harvard," she said, smiling. "I love you."

"Laura Lessoway." He held her tighter. "I love you, too." He kissed her, and it was both sad and happy, salty from the tears they'd cried and sweet.

A little while later, she looked at the man on the bed—his father. "Did you make it here on time?"

"I made it," he said. "We talked."

"Was it—I mean, did he... Did he know it was you?" She wanted, so badly, for Jonathan to have received some peace.

He nodded. "He knew."

"I'm so glad."

He picked up her hand. He kissed it. "I wouldn't have found him, if it wasn't for you. I would have waited, and it would have been too late."

She pressed her face into his neck again, her arms wrapping around him. "I'm sorry. I'm so, so sorry for your loss."

She held him for a few minutes, then disentangled herself and said, "So, your office. They said you're taking a sabbatical?"

He snorted. "I tried to quit. My boss didn't want me to. He told me to take the six weeks of vacation I have saved up and think about it. I said okay."

"Why'd you try to quit?"

He pressed his forehead to hers, his voice going rough and quiet. "Because I'm tired, Laura. I'm tired of giving everything to a job that doesn't give me anything back." He took a deep breath, put a hand on the side of her face. "I want to have a life. I want to have a life here, with you."

She closed her eyes against the mix of emotions that were tangled up in his gaze—tenderness, hope, fear, love. She felt something large and buoyant bubble up inside her. "You want to stay *here*, with me?"

"Yeah, I want to be with you and Emma. Really be with you. The way you want, and the way you deserve. I know you've been let down in the past, sweetheart, but *love* isn't an empty word to me. I'll be staying with Brett for the next six weeks. Let me show you what real love looks like, and if you still want me after that, I'll put in my notice and stay."

"Are you sure? Your partnership—"

He shook his head. "Was costing me too much. I thought my job could fulfill me, but it left me empty. You're what I need, Laura. You. And I know this happened fast and it might sound crazy, but I swear, I feel like I've been waiting for you my entire life."

She was crying again now, happy tears dripping down her face. What they wanted was the same. They wanted the same things, after all.

He leaned his forehead against hers again. He wiped the tears from her face. "Say something, sweetheart. Tell me you want me to stay."

She smiled and squeezed him tighter. Her heart felt like it would burst, it was so full. "I'd go anywhere for you, Harvard. Of course I want you to stay."

Epilogue

The Sea Glass Inn's summer season officially ended the second weekend in September. Laura and Emma had stayed until the very end, helping the chambermaids wash and fold bed linens, applying weather stripping to the windows in the guest rooms and packing up Gram's personal effects.

The summer had been a good one, businesswise—hot and not too rainy. The inn was full almost every weekend and usually close to capacity during the week. Laura had found that she liked running the inn on her own. She enjoyed getting up early and organizing the big continental breakfast. She liked hosting afternoon tea and watching the sun set over the dunes. She even liked the bookkeeping and the property maintenance, which—along with her burgeoning web design business—kept her busy during the long summer afternoons.

When Pastor Nate had approached her at the end of August and asked if she wanted to stay on as property manager once the church took possession of the inn, she'd gasped and grabbed Jonathan's hand. "You're not selling?"

The two men had exchanged a look. "We're going to keep it," Nate said. "Your grandmother and I talked about it before she died, and that's what we agreed. Plus, it's profitable, so it'll fund our outreach ministries. If you're amenable to working for room and board and a small stipend in the summer, there's really no downside for us."

"I thought for sure you'd sell it," she said.

Nate grinned. "Do you want the job?"

Laura shook her head, chuckling at the memory. Her grandmother would be happy with the outcome, she thought. They'd host church events at the inn, weddings and dances and retreats. Her mother didn't want to hear about it at all, but then again, when had she ever really wanted to hear much about Laura's life anyway? She was back in Hong Kong, and their relationship was in much the same place it had always been, though Laura felt better about it—she'd achieved some new level of acceptance, she supposed. She thought her grandmother would have been pleased about that, too.

After spending a few days in Upstate New York with his mother and sister, Jonathan had stayed at Brett's for the remainder of his six-week sabbatical, and then gone back to Boston for three months to finish up his work at the firm. Mike Roe, who had his hands full with the Carberry Hotels account, had taken full advantage of Jonathan's three-month notice period, working his protégé to the bone all summer. Even so, Jonathan had managed to drive down to Cape Cod to see her and Emma every weekend, and every once in a while, when Chloe and Brett were available to watch the inn, Laura and Emma had driven up to Boston midweek for a Red Sox game.

He'd moved back in with Brett after Labor Day, after his work at the law firm was done. Mike had used his connections to get Jonathan an interview with—and a subsequent job offer from—the Massachusetts Department of Children and Families, where he now served as a staff attorney in Barnstable County's Juvenile and Probate Court. Although the job paid *way* less than he'd been making before, it was significantly less time-consuming, and significantly more meaningful. Ethan Malone and Talia Morgan—from their new dorms at UMass—had sent him a singing telegram his first day on the job.

After his first week on Cape Cod full-time, he'd bought Emma a puppy, and he dropped by the inn every morning before work to help her daughter take the playful little Lab for a walk. He also came by for dinner most nights, after which he and Emma would walk the dog again, and sometimes fly a kite.

Laura couldn't remember ever feeling so happy. It was as though Jonathan's love had lit a lamp inside her, and now nothing could switch it off.

The first weekend in October was glorious, crisp, bright and sunny. Jonathan had biked over to the inn after lunch and lured Laura down to the beach with a rakish smile. "It's almost high tide," he said. "Know what that means?"

She arched an eyebrow, remembering their first time out on the jetty and the way the waves had soaked his suit pants, leaving giant salt stains. "That you need to go home and change into a suit?"

He laughed. "That would take too long. We'd miss it."

Hand in hand, they strolled down Sand Street Beach's rickety wooden boardwalk, steeping themselves in the sun. A handful of local kids ran by, jubilant as they chased a colorful kite. Seagulls squalled overhead and waves lapped the shore in a sibilant whisper, but Laura was struck most by the stillness of the afternoon. It was as though they were wrapped in a giant cloak of seclusion. The two of them against the world.

The waves weren't big, but the dark rocks of the jetty were still slick and sandy, the occasional shattered crab shell or splotch of bird poop dotting the path.

Halfway to the end, Laura turned around and smiled at Jonathan, her hair unruly although there was hardly any wind to whip it out of shape. "You're getting better at this," she teased.

He grinned. "Practice makes perfect." They'd made a habit of walking to the lighthouse and back every Sunday afternoon all summer—most of the time with Emma, although her daughter had stayed home with Chloe and Brett today.

At the end of the jetty they sat with their backs against the small lighthouse, looking out to sea. Laura nestled her head on Jonathan's shoulder, and he smoothed his hand over her hair. She could have stayed out there with her head on his shoulder forever, breathing with the rise of his chest, witnessed by the light and the waves and the gulls.

After a time, Jonathan shifted, reaching for something in his pocket.

Laura felt her stomach lurch, though her heart was soft and expectant.

And then it was happening: the velvet box in his hand, him kneeling in front of her, the expression on his face hopeful, and vulnerable, and a little bit scared.

"You're everything I've ever wanted, Laura, and you make me so incredibly happy. Will you marry me?"

"Oh, Jonathan," she whispered, vaguely aware that he'd popped the lid of the ring box open, but too consumed with happiness to look. "Yes!"

A sound of joy and relief escaped him, and then he had her in his arms, hugging her, squeezing her, lifting her off the ground.

"Careful!" She laughed and clutched him tightly—they were awfully close to the edge.

"Don't worry," he said. "I'd never let you go."

He set her back on her feet and took her left hand. It was shaking. He slipped an antique emerald engagement ring with distinctive three-leaf shoulders onto her finger. "Gram's ring!" she cried, her voice full of wonder. "Where did you get this?"

"Your grandmother left it with Nate for safekeeping. He was supposed to give it to you when you took over the inn, but I convinced him to let me give it to you instead."

Laura stared at her hand in disbelief. The emerald wasn't big—it was less than a carat—but it was clear and vibrant. The small diamonds in the leaves on the sides shone dazzlingly in the sun, and the millegrain edgework on the band was delicate and fine.

"We can get you something more modern if you'd like."

"Not on your life! It's beautiful," she said fiercely. "Exactly what I wanted."

"*You're* beautiful."

She swatted him playfully on the chest. "Flattery will get you everywhere."

"That's what I'm hoping," he said, "because I've got one more surprise for you." He took an envelope out of his back pocket. "Up for some ice cream?"

She opened the envelope and laughed. "Pretty sure of yourself there, Harvard." It was an invitation to their engagement party. At The Sundae School. Tonight.

He smiled and gave her a playful tap on the nose. "Optimistic, I'd say. Hopeful. And desperately, madly in love with you."

She grinned at him and went up on her tiptoes, sliding her arms around his neck. "You don't say?"

In response, he circled her waist with his hands and kissed her. Then he released her waist but tugged at her hand. "Well, come on, Mrs. Soon-to-Be-Masters. Party starts at six, and Tiny needs her ice cream. We haven't got all day."

She laughed. She let him lead her off the jetty. He was her fiancé now, her family. She would follow him anywhere he wanted to go.

* * * * *

If you enjoyed this book,
be sure to check out these other titles:

Child on His Doorstep
by Lee Tobin McClain

Raising Honor
by Jill Lynn

Ready to Trust
by Tina Radcliffe

The Orphans' Blessing
by Lorraine Beatty

Available now from Love Inspired!

Find more great reads at www.LoveInspired.com.

Dear Reader,

I hope you enjoyed your trip to The Sea Glass Inn in the fictional town of Wychmere Bay, Cape Cod! I grew up spending my summers at a cozy Cape Cod inn a lot like this one—one that my mother and her sisters still own to this day!

More than the setting, though, I hope you enjoyed Laura and Jonathan's journey. These characters and their struggles are dear to my heart, and I am beyond humbled that God chose me to tell their story.

So often, we pick up false beliefs in childhood that we unconsciously carry with us into adulthood. For Laura, the idea that she isn't good enough for lasting love makes her doubt her own instincts. For Jonathan, who's been scarred by his father's battle with mental illness, the idea that he can "earn" the life he wants by achieving great things in his career means that he's never even entertained the possibility of falling in love.

I'm thrilled that Laura and Jonathan were able to find happiness with each other. I pray that you, too, will seek help for anything that's holding you back from becoming the person God wants you to be.

Wishing you love and light,
Meghann

SPECIAL EXCERPT FROM

LOVE INSPIRED
INSPIRATIONAL ROMANCE

*When a television reporter must go into hiding,
she finds a haven deep in Amish country.
Could she fall in love with the simple life—
and a certain Amish man?*

Read on for a sneak preview of
The Amish Newcomer *by Patrice Lewis.*

"Isaac, we have a visitor. This is Leah Porte. She's an *Englischer* friend of ours, staying with us a few months. Leah, this is Isaac Sommer."

For a moment Isaac was struck dumb by the newcomer. With her dark hair tamed back under a *kapp*, and her chocolate eyes, he barely noticed the ugly red scar bisecting her right cheek.

Leah stepped forward. "How do you do?"

"Fine, *danke*. Where do you come from?"

"California."

"Please, sit. Both of you." Edith Byler gestured toward the table.

Isaac found himself opposite Leah and gazed at her as the family gathered around the table. When all heads bowed in silence, he found himself praying he could get to know the visitor better.

At once, chatter broke out as the family reached for food.

"We hope you'll have a pleasant stay with us." Ivan Byler scooped corn onto his plate .

"I…I'm not familiar with your day-to-day life." The woman toyed with her fork. "I don't want to be seen as a freeloader."

"What is it you did before you came here?" Ivan asked.

"I was a television journalist," she replied. Isaac saw her touch her wounded cheek and glance toward him. "But after my…my car accident, I couldn't do my job anymore."

Journalist! What kind of God-sent coincidence was that? He smiled. "Maybe I should have you write some articles for my magazine."

"Magazine?"

Edith explained, "Isaac started a magazine for Plain people. He uses a computer to create it. The bishop gave him permission."

"An Amish man using a computer?"

"Many *Englischers* have misconceptions of how much technology the *Leit* allows," Ivan intervened. "You won't find computers in our homes, or cell phones. But while we try to live not *of* the world, we still live *in* the world, and sometimes technology is needed to keep our businesses running. So, some bishops have decided a little technology is allowed."

"What's the magazine about?" Leah asked.

"Whatever appeals to Plain people. Farming. Businesses. Land management."

"And you want *me* to write for it?" she asked. "I don't know anything about those topics."

"But that's what a journalist does, ain't so? Learn about new topics," Isaac replied. Her opposition made him more determined. "Besides, you're about to get a crash course while you stay here. Maybe you'll learn something."

"I already said I had no intention of being a freeloader."

He nodded. "*Gut.* Then prove it. You can write me an article about what you learn."

"Sure," she snapped. "How hard could it be?"

He grinned. "You'll find out soon enough."

Don't miss
The Amish Newcomer *by Patrice Lewis,*
available September 2020 wherever
Love Inspired books and ebooks are sold.

LoveInspired.com

LIEXP0820

LOVE INSPIRED
INSPIRATIONAL ROMANCE

IS LOOKING FOR NEW AUTHORS!

Do you have an idea for an inspirational
contemporary romance book?

Do you enjoy writing faith-based romances about small-town
men and women who overcome challenges and fall in love?

We're looking for new authors for Love Inspired,
and we want to see your story!

Check out our writing guidelines and
submit your Love Inspired manuscript at
Harlequin.com/Submit

CONNECT WITH US AT:

www.LoveInspired.com

Facebook.com/LoveInspiredBooks

Twitter.com/LoveInspiredBks

Facebook.com/groups/HarlequinConnection